LOVERS IN DEEP
THE SEA MEN, BOOK 3

DANI STOWE

BABE FUEL
BOOKS.COM

The Sea Men

∾

Edited by Kim Burger

∾

WARNING: This book contains material that may not be suitable for all readers due to its sexual content, graphic imagery, and some violence.

∾

All rights reserved © 2018 Babe Fuel Books; 2017 by Dani Stowe. This is a work of fiction. All of the characters, organizations, and events portrayed in this novel are either products of the author's imagination or are used fictitiously. Any resemblance to actual persons, living or dead, actual events or locales is purely coincidental.

∾

This book or any portion thereof may not be reproduced or used in any manner without the express written permission of the author. This e-book may also not be re-sold, transferred, or given to other people without written permission of the author.

❈ Created with Vellum

PROLOGUE

ATHENA

Fifteen Years Old...
"How are you today, Captain?" I push a long strand of my wavy brown hair behind my ear where the temple tips of my glasses rest and I peer into the calm, still water. "Nothing to say?" I ask, waiting for any sign of life.

Nothing stirs.

All I see is murky ocean blue with a hint of green under the bright midday sun.

"Hmph." He can hide all he wants to, but beneath the surface, I know he's there.

With one finger, I push up on the bridge of my glasses that have run down to the tip of my nose. "I guess I'll do all the talking," I smirk. "*As usual.*"

As I maneuver to sit crisscross, the small boat with a small engine wobbles.

"I've had a long year," I say to the water as I grab a pencil and my sketchbook atop a thick book of fairytales.

I sketch the eyes that have haunted my dreams since I was a small child, but not in a nightmarish kind of way. I draw

1

them big and masculine, but soft, and shadow them a light gray.

"A boy asked me to the senior prom this year," I mention. "Can you believe it? A *senior* asked me, a *freshman*, to prom. He's a bit of a nerd, but Mom was still really upset that I declined. Do you know what a nerd is?" I bite the end of the pencil to gnaw on the eraser and spit when I notice I'm about to swallow the rubber. I scratch my head. "Do you even know what *prom* is?"

I lean to look over the boat.

Nothing. But I do notice myself, my golden eyes looking back this time.

"It's a dance," I explain to my reflection, "but you know I could not attend because... well... fish don't dance. Which reminds me, I overheard Mom talking to Dad the other day. They are considering getting me some psychotherapy, but my grade point average is high, so my regular doctor has been trying to convince them that my imagination is just the result of high brain activity." I laugh. "But you and I both know that *you* are not imaginary."

I go back to my drawing. The water is calm today. But then again, it's always calm when I come to visit during the summers.

"I made a friend," I announce. "She's an older lady. Cora Morae. I ran into her at the grocery in town while with my parents. She told them I had a particular aura about me—said it was 'magical.' She invited my parents and me to dine with her at her beach house. She mentioned having a niece, younger than me, who lives with her that she'd like for us to meet. Ms. Morae also wants to take us on a hike across one of her properties, which rests at the edge of a bay. She says the scenery is quite beautiful and at certain times of the year you can see..." My cheeks rise. *"Meeeeermen,"* I slur.

The boat sways.

Oh, my gosh! He's finally stirring. I feel giddy.

"Ms. Morae says she's an expert on merfolk. Not only did she tell me how to summon a sea witch in our short meeting, but she even told me how to summon a *mermaid*, although she says there haven't been one of those for centuries. You simply call to her by her divine name—whatever *that* means."

The boat sways again, turning. The front drifts to point towards the shore and I notice a small wave coming in from behind me.

My giddiness is sinking!

I drop my drawing pad and pencil to lean over the boat, pleading. "Please, I didn't mean to upset you."

A splash of cool water droplets fly across my shoulders and I turn to see the small wave has landed against the back end of my boat, thrusting. My hair flies out of my face as the wave pushes me, taking me back to shore. The ride is smooth and *fun!* I feel like I'm on a never-ending slide. Butterflies float in my belly as I glide across the sea's surface, but sadness sweeps over me as land creeps closer.

I've upset him. I mentioned mermen, which I often do, but this time I also mentioned mermaids and he's not amused. Per my research, I suspect he has no access to the opposite gender of any kind and so perhaps I've insulted him since he's taking me back to shore.

Shortly, I find myself being splashed tremendously as the boat is nudged repeatedly. Short wave after short wave slams against the back, forcing the boat onto the beach and when I'm fairly stuck in the sand, just slightly past the shoreline, the waves retract.

I turn around to face the open ocean. It's nearly flat again. Only the tiniest waves unfurl across the beach. Getting out of the boat, I pick up my notepad and pencil once more. Stomping through the sand until my toes hit the water, I *kick* at the sea, causing a spray but again...

Nothing.

Mermen, I think and hold up the notepad, fixing the sketch directly in front of my face.

Looking into the eyes I've drawn, the eyes I suspect belong to a great sea captain transformed by magic, I tilt my head to look at the sea beyond.

Cradling my sketchpad in my arms, I make a note: **He's real.**

1

WILLIS

*L*ove.

I've never known love. At least, not the kind my brothers have to come to know.

It seems to be a lot of work this love. Look at all the trouble the lads have been forced to endure for the sake of such silliness, for the sake of...

Women.

I should say I like women and I do recall enjoying everything about them—the scent, the feel. I miss the tender stroke of soft hands upon my body, the gritty tendrils of long hair getting caught in my mouth, and the hot blow of steam that entered my body right before soft lips would press into my own.

I miss being inside a woman. The feel of hips in my palms as I gripped her frail, warm body, especially while I took her from behind.

I smile to myself. It's not really a smile. I have no mouth, but I can almost feel the corners of what I remember to be a mouth bend and my cupid bow spreading as the fleshy plump center of my bottom lip stretches while my facial cheeks rise and flush.

Mmm, I miss smiling and I miss having the opportunity to make a pretty girl smile at me as well.

Except this one—the *librarian*.

Yes, I know all about her. *How can I not?* She's obsessed with me. The woman won't leave me alone.

I saved her life once when she was child and one would think that after such a traumatic experience, the girl, now a woman, would either forget or never be inclined to dip so much as a toe back into the ocean.

But not this one.

Nooo.

This one thinks she has some special connection to the sea. To me.

I am reluctant to reminisce of our first encounter, but I remember her as a child twenty-seven years ago...

Where are her parents? Damn them! I thought.

The small child peeped over the edge of the boat and

though my body no longer possessed a physical human state, with the exception of my eyes, I still felt an uneasy sensation.

The little girl wrapped her tiny fingers around a post as her fat feet popped over the edge. She leaned her head through an opening under the railing. If I didn't do something, she was going to fall in!

I couldn't rock the boat to get her parents' attention or the child would've surely fallen, sunk, and drown. I swiftly made my way around the boat looking for any sign of the child's parents so that perhaps I could get their attention with a splash, but they were nowhere to be seen.

A soft thud shook the water, which ran through me followed by a second thud and a third. It was coming from the interior of the small vessel. *Those parents had left their child unattended to get intimate!*

I went back to the child. She's was hanging halfway over.

"Fishy," she called out, reaching towards the blue abyss that would swallow her whole if I didn't do something.

I thought, *Perhaps if I scare her!* Then she would not be so inclined to take the leap.

I positioned myself directly beneath her so she could see my stormy gray eyes. They were the only pieces of my human body I'd been left with since being transformed by magic into nothing but a mass of seawater.

The child was more than two-thirds of the way over the edge at that point. Her fine sun-kissed honey color tendrils of wavy shoulder-length hair were hanging over her face and the ends brushed across the surface of the water to tickle me with worry.

I showed her meaner eyes, popping myself out as a glob of water, giving her a wicked glare—but the child smiled!

Silly girl. Stop smiling! I wished her mother would show to spank her.

She reached with her fingers to poke me in the eye. The

sensation was so overwhelming, I was both shocked and stunned. I wanted to move but I couldn't.

I let the child's tiny fingers poke me in the eye again. The scrape of her bitty nail dug into my orbs and it hurt but I didn't back away. It was the first time in over two hundred years I'd had any genuine human contact, so I allowed myself to experience the slight scrape and sting of her tiny fingers. I had no idea I'd missed being touched, even if it was painful. It was the only place I could feel any type of pressing sensation.

A small drop—no, it was a tear—flowed from my eye then spread across the surface of the water to become a grander ripple of waves that rocked the boat, and the child *fell in!*

Down she went, plummeting straight into the depths of the sea. I looked about to see if her parents were even aware that their innocent little girl had slipped so easily away from them. She was far below the surface and if I'd had a heart, I admit it would have beat painfully for the little thing. She was so small and without any ability to swim.

I sensed her motions. She was kicking profusely but making very little turbulence with her flailing little hands, arms, and chubby legs.

Ducking down to her level in the deep blue, I swirled about her. Her panicking eyes followed my own eyes and she reached for me.

Could she not see I had no arms, no legs, no body?

Her eyes got big then. They were *huge*, glaring back at me. I felt a twist in my transparent gut once more.

It was not like me to get involved in human matters. I warned myself against saving the child. After what had happened aboard the Annabelle, I swore I would never attempt another rescue. The failed attempt to save that witch was the reason I am in the form I am in now.

I promised myself that I would never get involved with

LOVERS IN DEEP

humans, except of course when Poseidon, himself, demands it because I have no choice. The powers with which I've been bestowed are beyond destructive—they are evil. The immense strength and mass I possess has the potential to destroy whole cities and villages. With a simple stir, I can force the ocean to swallow an entire island whole, along with all its inhabitants.

I sensed the child swallow. It was a big gulp and she began sinking more quickly, so it was only a matter of time. I'd observed drownings thousands of times. The child's pulse was racing. I could feel the chambers of her heart slamming against the interior walls of the blood pumping organ creating its own tiny ripple of small waves to vibrate through me.

I looked up once more towards the boat above. The child's parents were still unaware that she was missing and I felt the child's heart begin to slow.

I looked back to her, expecting to see a face filled with dread, looking pitiful, and desperate for saving, but the child's eyes were filled with contempt.

She was angry with me. She was on the brink of death, and *she was angry!*

I'd seen that anger, that conviction many times in the eyes of my sea mates, my brothers, and it pulled at my heart-strings. I almost felt as though I had a heart again.

With my powers, I forced a wave to swirl beneath her, circling and circling, until she was spinning and choking. I kept her on the very brink of death because I wanted her to learn a very valuable lesson. I didn't ever want her to go overboard again. I wanted her to know the consequences of what it meant to fall into the deep. And when I sensed her heart could no longer keep up with her angry mind, I pushed her upward to the sky.

Bursting into the air, the child went atop a shooting fountain where she gagged and coughed then cleared her throat until she was rolling in what appeared to be delight.

Ugh. That child! She was laughing, despite the near-death experience.

With a constant stream of spouting water, I floated the child back onto the boat.

My aim was not perfect and she landed face first where she grumbled but came to standing as I retracted my reach.

"Athena!" shouted a woman, her mother.

Finally!

"Oh, my dear," her mother cried. "What happened to you? You're all wet!"

A rumble echoed through me as the boat ignited, spinning the propeller at the rear.

As the boat took off, I saw lightning in the distance. My brother, Henry, must've been at work.

I should not have saved the child. I was not a witch or a fortune teller, but it was obvious this girl seemed doomed. But since I'd already made a rescue, I decided I'd better stay with her for a bit longer to ensure smooth sailing considering the storm ahead. Of course, I didn't need to, but I figured I should at least accompany her until she made it back to shore since I had already wasted so much energy.

After that day, I prayed to the gods that child would forever be in fear of the sea. I hoped she would never again attempt another dive in or another drowning...

But look at Athena now. She is behaving as she always has—trying to get me to reveal myself. Day after day she comes to visit me.

I'd love to tell her she's not my type. Her nose is too pointy and her legs are too thin. I despise thin legs. They have no place at sea, so no place among seamen.

And those spectacles? The ones she must constantly adjust to stay up her nose. Those things are bigger than her tiny pair of breasts. I like *big* breasts. Bosoms that hang out the sides of my palms.

If I could laugh at her I would. Just look at her. Running to me out of that flimsy blue hut the rest of the seamen have shacked up in. It would take but a small splash for me to knock that thing over.

"Willis!" Athena calls.

Athena. She doesn't deserve a name like that, the divine name of a most magnificent goddess, though Athena's persistence does deserve at minimum some retrospect.

Athena has been chasing me for a long time. She brings

her contraptions and her books. Sometimes she will row her boat to greet me, often too far from the shore for my liking.

Other times, she simply sits on the beach and reads to me—the legends and folklore that have convinced her of my existence. It makes me feel sorry for her, really.

The girl has been so preoccupied with me and the other seamen throughout the whole of her existence that I've yet to see her in the company of the opposite gender. I wonder if she's yet to have ever found herself in the arms of a lover.

It saddens me—though only slightly—to think I am the cause of Athena's loneliness. And I wonder, *does she not know she is lonely?*

Though I'm hardly attracted to her, I suppose if I had legs and arms I might indulge her. If I were the man, the *Captain*, that I was, I would most certainly give her a taste of all that she has given up for the sake of her scholarly quests.

"Willis!" she shouts to me again from the beach.

It makes no sense to hide from Athena now. She's already entangled herself in the business of magic and the other seamen. She knows all about us and our past. I shall admit, she is a clever creature.

"Willis!" she stomps her foot in the sand.

I'm surprised at the tiny thing—calling to me so demandingly. *Is she not afraid of the wall—the tidal wave—that I am in front of her?* I could easily crush her, *kill* her instantly! Or, sweep about her skinny legs and drown her with a slow death.

I splash her by shooting a spray of water at her and she gasps.

Oh, the look on her face. I wish I could laugh. She's stunned now—her mouth is open and her face has paled as it drips of seawater.

Her breasts peep through the top of the wet fabric.

Mmm, she certainly has grown. She's clearly not a child

anymore. For whatever reason, it excites me to want to play with her some more.

I shoot another stream of water at her again and she squeals, becoming stiff with the shock of having been soaked.

Oh, if I had a body it would be rolling in the sand, unable to remain upright with such tremendous laughter. I'm confident this is not what Athena had envisioned how a first meet with the *Captain of all the Seas* to be.

Hmm...

She's sulking now, removing her spectacles to shake the water away. Her bottom lip quivers as she sucks it in.

Perhaps I should not have shot at her a second time. I can sense a bit of dense salty fluid. Tears are spilling from Athena's eyes.

I suppose despite her scholarly appearance, which is hardly attractive, Athena has pretty eyes. I know how fierce, determined, and gentle those eyes can be at different times. Eyes like those should not be so sad.

I suppose I should also leave her be. I do wish she would leave *me* be. In light of all her collected scholarly material, Athena has yet to learn there is no hope for me. I wish desperately for her to understand this. I have been cursed to command the seas for all eternity. And one day, Athena will be nothing more than a silly girl in a lost memory.

2

ATHENA

The sea has gone flat again. The Captain has sailed away, sneaking off to the vastness of the ocean, and it breaks my heart.

Shelley comes shouting from the beach house, "Athena! Are you okay?" Her fingers grip my elbow.

"Why does he do that?" I wipe my wet face and flick the saltwater from my fingers. "Why won't he show himself to me?"

"I think he showed himself to you the best he could," says Orphelius, approaching and giving me a look over. "We should be glad he didn't drown us."

I pull off my glasses and rub them the best I can to clear the lenses from blobs of water, but my shirt is wet as well. All I do is smear the lenses with streaks. "Do you really think he'd do that?" I glower at Orphelius. "You think he'd kill us?"

"All that studying, Athena, you've been doing on mermen and magic. *Us*. *Him*." Orphelius scratches his jaw. "You have no idea who he really is, do you?"

"I know he's your friend. You're like a brother to him, are

you not? The folktales talk of Captain Willis as though he is a good man, a *great* man," I correct myself.

"Mmm, a great man he once was," Orphelius nods and bites his lip before his eyes gloss over the ocean. "But that was before we were tossed into the ocean, into the great abyss where our Captain became the very thing he once loved to sail upon. The sea may seem calm from where we stand right now but believe me when I say below lurks many demons and they all belong to him—*his* demons."

A siren sounds from beyond the beach house and we each turn our backs to the ocean.

"Shelley!" a voice yells. It's Sheriff Pike.

We make our way up the beach back to the house and I notice Henry wheels himself out to the top of the ramp.

Shelley runs up the beach. "What do you want?" She yells nastily as Pike comes walking around the corner and Orphelius and I run after her. We are all thinking the same thing, hoping Pike is not here to cause more trouble despite being a man of the law.

"I just want to talk to all of you," Pike has his hands up, away from his gun, but he's got his eyes on Henry.

Shelley's also got her hands up and she pushes on Pike's chest. She's not going to let the sheriff pass. "Go away! You have no business coming here."

"Now, that's not true. I still have a case unsolved—your *parents'* case—and as the sheriff of this town, it's my duty to seek justice. Now, I've been thinking about this for a while. I thought about you and your fish friend." The sheriff nudges his chin at Henry in his chair and then swallows. "I thought about you all a lot for the few days I was locked up in that crazy psyche ward, which they attributed my actions to a midlife crisis, and I even let you have some time to yourselves, but *Goddamn it*, Shelley. This is *my* town! I've protected it for a long time. I take a lot of pride in knowing all that goes on here and between the poachers, strange weather, and crazy critters, I've always suspected your Aunt Cora might've been right. I always had a feeling this town was cursed with all the unexplained hocus pocus going around, but I've got real problems right now. Problems that I need to solve. I got missing girls, two teenagers, both of whom disappeared this week. Now, I don't know what happened to your parents," Pike looks to Henry again, "but I still have evidence that says your friend there was involved. So, I need the truth, Shelley, because right now, your transforming fish friend is still my number one suspect."

Henry signs with his hands furiously and Shelley pauses, kicking the sand. She finally nods to herself, crossing her arms before she looks back to Pike. "Would you like to hear a tale, Sheriff?"

The sheriff points a finger and shakes his head at Henry. "Young man, I don't want no tall tales."

"Young man?" laughs Orphelius. "I assure you, Sheriff, our tales are not tall but they are old. We are much, much older than you."

"Mmm," grunts the sheriff, rubbing his jaw. "So, you're one of them, too, huh?"

Orphelius smiles and nods.

"Ugh," growls the sheriff. "I shoulda known anyone shacking up in Cora Morae's house would be different."

Kumiko steps out the door, leaning up against the back of Henry's chair. "Oh, hey," she looks surprised to see Pike here. "What's going on? Orphelius, you told me to stay put, but when you didn't come back—"

"She one of them, too?" asks the sheriff, examining Kumiko. "One of you, *creatures*? She's got to be one."

Orphelius laughs. "No, Kumiko is human."

Henry cocks his head, grabs his wheels, and turns his chair around then signs.

Shelley translates, "Henry wants to invite you in."

The sheriff puts his hand on the handle of his gun. "I'm not going to get any trouble from you, am I?"

Shelley calmly places her hand on the sheriff's forearm and it surprisingly seems to calm him. "Pike, Henry just wants to sit down."

Pike rubs his jaw. "Sit down, huh?"

Henry flashes a modest but genuine smile and holds out an open palm towards the door.

Shelley translates again. "He says it's time for you all to chat. Chat like *real* men."

I hate that I'm pouting. The corners of my mouth can't seem to deviate from their downward spiral and I also hate that everyone keeps looking at me. As Henry professes his role in Shelley's parents' deaths, the rest—Kumiko and Orphelius won't stop frowning at me as they pity me.

Shelley was nice enough to grab me a towel before she sat to translate because I'm drenched. Willis splashed... or sprayed... or more like *squirted* water at me.

It's embarrassing.

Orphelius cuts in during Henry's tale to explain their magical pasts and the sheriff is still having difficulty coming to grips with each seaman's story. In truth, the sheriff appears at odds with himself—both intrigued and upset with disbelief. I remember Shelley wore the same look on her face before she could finally accept Henry for who and what he truly was.

I look through the bay window as we are all sitting around the table and for the first time *ever*, I'm regretting having ever believed. In magic. In merpeople. In mermen.

I've spent many summers with the sea and as soon as I became an adult and could afford to move out on my own after college, I saved money so I could move back to this town. I always thought I was connected to this place somehow. I always thought it was the place where I would officially meet my destiny one day.

Like a foolish girl, I'd believed that I was special, that there were secrets the sea would only reveal to me, like the fact that it was a living entity that moved because it was willed to do so and that it could see with eyes once only shown to me.

I also believed the sea could speak. I'd observed bubbles rising, popping open at the surface to release gossip and whispers from the mouths of fish that often swarmed beneath my boat. Not once did I doubt my beliefs. And I've been doing everything in my power to protect those beliefs, no matter how critical or harsh people were to me.

A chill passes through my body and I pull the towel tighter around my shoulders.

Orphelius is glaring at me now. He sends me a flat grin, which I believe is intended to make me feel better but it feels more like an I-told-you-so.

The Captain has no interest in me. Willis revealed himself

as a massive wall of water and the second I ran out to face him, he squirted me. And it wasn't just once but *twice,* like I'm the silly target of some carnival water gun game.

I look at Shelley and Kumiko and they are beautiful. Just beautiful. One is fair with strawberry-colored hair while the other seems rare due to her sharply angled exotic features as a result of her mixed heritage. I recognize that Shelley and Kumiko are the specimens from which fairytales are made. It's why their mermen are so captivated by them, willing to fight, chase after, and even die for them.

But me?

"Ah, me," I sigh, which causes Henry to pause his hand speech and look forlornly in my direction—another reminder that I'm not worth a merman.

Jeez, am I really that pathetic?

I get up.

"Hey, where are you going?" asks the sheriff.

"Back to the library," I tell him.

"Listen, Athena," Pike points at me. "I know how late you like to lock yourself up with those books at night and then leave when there's not a soul around. I don't want you doing that anymore. I want that library locked up at least an hour before sunset and I want you in your home before dark."

I laugh, "Sheriff—"

He stands up. "I'm not kidding around, Athena. And I don't want to see you seaside at midnight, either. I know you like to check those books out, plant yourself alone in the dark on the beach, and read aloud with your flashlight like you're tellin' tales to these merfolk."

Oh crap! The sheriff knows about that?

"You read to Willis at night?" asks Orphelius, his brows furrowed.

I blush. "Nnnnno." I don't know why I'm denying it. I'm still embarrassed I guess that Willis squirted me in front of everyone. Clearly, Willis doesn't like me and I feel foolish for having believed that he was listening to me for all these years, which I now figure he wasn't.

"Athena, whatever it is you're doing out there at night, I need you to keep off the beach." Pike points to Shelley and Kumiko as well. "And that goes for the rest of you. I got two girls gone missin' from what looks like two different beach locations, so I'm not ruling out kidnapping. And until I figure out what's going on, the beaches will be closed after dark."

"Sheriff," I interject, "closing the beaches at night is going to upset a lot of people. We have tourists plus fisherman who like to go out at night and—"

"I don't care," he growls. "And since you're heading back to the library, make me a hundred or so signs on your copy machine. Make sure the print is clear: Streets and beaches close at sunset by my order. I'll come by to pick those up tomorrow and put 'em up. Can you do that for me, Athena?"

Two girls—*missing.* My eyes wander towards the horizon over the sea and I wonder if Captain Willis would be able to help in getting answers, but I quickly toss the idea out of my mind. Willis is not the type to communicate.

"Yeah," I nod to Pike as I remove the wet towel from around my shoulders and hand it over to Shelley with a thankful grin. "I'll have those copies for you this afternoon, Sheriff."

3

ATHENA

Seagulls are perched atop the library. There has to be at least fifty of them up there and I get the feeling that they're all looking at me—spying with their curiously tilted heads and blinking eyes.

"Go away! Shoo," I shout and they all squawk at one another in a cawing chorus with their feathery bellies bellowing with laughter while remaining exactly where they are.

I sigh as I pull out the keys to the library and notice the door is slightly ajar.

Strange. I know I locked this. At least, I think I did.

I push the heavy wooden door open just slightly and poke my head inside and then pause.

Missing girls. It's a scary thought and I consider that perhaps I should call the sheriff, but I also wonder why anyone related to what the sheriff suspects as kidnapping would have anything to do with the library. I'm sure there's nothing to worry about but I'm still cautious as I inch my way in through the door.

There's some fumbling going on. I can hear it. It's coming

from behind the checkout counter and, since I can't see who it is, I figure it's a kid or two.

"Hey!" I shout, pushing the heavy wooden door wide open as I march towards the counter. "What are you doing? Get out from there."

A head with black hair hosting light green eyes pops up, which is not at all what I suspected. "I-I-I'm sorry," the tall, slender young man stutters as he blinks blankly at me behind thick black frames. He pushes his glasses up his nose and looks me up and down.

We study one another.

He looks innocent and... *cute*.

A smile plays on his mouth.

My heart palpates—heavily.

My cheeks warm—rapidly.

He interrupts the static in the room. "The doors were open," he says, his pearly whites coming fully exposed as he hoists a couple of books onto the counter. "I was hoping to check these out but since no one was in here, I figure I'd leave a note or something."

"Oh," I blink. "Um..." I can barely talk.

What's wrong with me!

He tilts his head. "Are you okay?"

"I'm okay," I exhale.

He chuckles. "Why are you all wet?"

Wet? Oh damn! I'm scrambling for an excuse. I certainly can't tell him a merman made mostly of water decided to squirt me.

"Oh," I laugh, "some kid got me with his water gun."

"Well, that sounds like fun," he chuckles again and his white, button up palm tree printed shirt sways over his straight, hip-hugging blue jeans, which makes me wish I could sway him myself. "Have you seen the librarian?" he asks.

"Librarian?" I mutter in a daze but the title snaps me back

to reality. "Yes! Oh, yes." I plant my hands over my chest. *"I'm the librarian."*

"You?" he looks me up and down once more. "You're too pretty to be a librarian. Are you sure?"

I'm blushing again. "Mhm."

"Soooo, can you check me out?" He bites his bottom lip and I figure he's got to be younger than me, perhaps visiting from the university.

Hopefully, he's not too *much younger.*

"I can check you out."

What? What did I just say? Idiot!

"I mean I can check out your *books*." Despite the coolness of my wet clothes, I think I'm perspiring.

"Great." He shrugs, his cheeks rising upward, touching the lower rims of his glasses.

We both walk to swap places and as I make my way around, heading to the opposite side of the counter, he comes in front, both of us batting our eyes at one another.

"How old are you?" he asks, leaning over the counter.

I'm ashamed to tell him. "Thirty."

He slams his hands on the counter. "Thirty? No way!" he exclaims. "I thought twenty-two or twenty-three. *Maybe*. Gosh, you're pretty."

I drop the first book I have in my hand and fumble to pick it back up. "You don't have to say that," I mutter, trying to collect myself. For a cute nerd, he sure is forward.

"Well, it's true." He cocks his head. "I was checking you out as you were walking past. You don't have a single scar on you and I like your skin tone."

My skin tone? Odd, especially since I'm sure my skin just flushed red.

"Can I see you under your glasses?" he asks.

I laugh, scanning the first book and placing it down to

pick up then flip through the second, a similarly themed book on sea navigation with maps included.

"C'mon," he smiles. "I'll take off mine if you take off yours."

"That's not necessary," I shake my head. I come to the conclusion he's got to be much younger than I am considering the way he's behaving.

"You married? Got a boyfriend?"

"Mmm..." I hestitate. I typically hesitate whenever I've been asked this question in the past and right now, I'm asking myself why I do that. But I'm more curious as to why I'm *not* married or *don't* have a boyfriend.

Because of Willis? Because I was saving myself for him? Silly woman.

"No. I don't have anyone."

"Great, so..."

He's checking me out again.

"If I take you out to dinner tonight, will you show me your face without your glasses on later?"

Dinner? I can't remember the last time I got asked out to dinner, though my mother says it's because I always have my face in a book.

I scan the second book from the stack and pick up the third. It's an old book about rigging—the proper use of ropes and chains for support during sailing. It looks like a book made for Boy Scouts. I glare up at him. "How old are you?"

He widens his stance, which is irritatingly sexy, and shoves both hands in his pockets. "Twenty-three."

"Mmm," escapes my mouth as my head drops.

"Listen, librarian," he picks up my head with a grip of his fingers wrapped under my chin, forcing our eyes to meet. "It's just dinner and, you know, I'm new here."

"Yes, I know." *Heavens, my knees are weak from the touch of his hands on my face and the way he called me "librarian"—slow and with a roll of the "r" on his tongue. I really want to hear him say it again.*

He tilts his head sexily sideways. His hands slip back in his pockets as if he has something to hide. *Naughty boy.* "So, who better than the town librarian to show me around?" he asks.

I perk up. "I'm also the town historian."

"No way!" He's so excited. "So, you can give me the scoop on everything here?"

"Mhm," I nod. "And I also work for the sheriff. I'm sort of his assistant."

He clears his throat and shoves his hands deeper in his back pockets. "Really? That's... that's quite fascinating. So, are you also a part of law enforcement? Do you carry a gun and all that stuff?"

"Oh, no." I roll my eyes. "I just do all of the sheriff's dirty work."

"Dirty work?" The young man is intrigued. "What kind of dirty work?"

"Not dirty," I correct myself. "It was a euphemism. I'm more of a bookkeeper. I keep our sheriff's files and evidence organized and clean up after him when I need to."

"Wow, you are one very interesting lady," he leans over the counter, takes off his glasses, and bats his eyes.

Damn! He is just as cute without the glasses as he is with them on, and I figure those fluttering lashes are an indication he's flirting with me but he just called me 'interesting' which doesn't sound very enticing. Perhaps if he had called me intriguing or beautiful or—

"Listen, sexy. I want to take you out. And I'm not the kind of guy you're going to have to clean up after. I promise." He cocks his head with a grimace and points at me. "What time do you get off?"

A hot nerd just called me sexy and he wants to take me out!

"I'll be closing up early per the sheriff's orders. About six."

"Per the sheriff, huh?"

"Yeah."

"Fascinating," he nods, slipping his glasses back on. "So, I'll be back at six to pick you up?"

"You can pick me up at the bakery down the road. Perhaps at seven?" I smile.

"All righty then," he snaps his fingers and fists one hand into the other, then points his fingers, like guns, at me and turns towards the doors.

"Hey, wait! What's your name?" I shout.

"My name?" He turns back with narrowed eyes. He looks curiously dangerous at this moment.

"I don't... know... yo-your name," I stutter.

"It's Levi. And yours?"

"Athena."

"Of course," he says with a chortle though it's mostly to himself. "With so many wonderful attributes, you just had to be a goddess. Didn't you? *Athena*." He growls my name as if he's hungry—like a wolf before it pounces on its prey, but then he bows his head down, his eyes glaring devilishly up at me through his glasses. "This is going to be a lot of fun, isn't it? I'll see you later." He waves and walks out, shutting the door behind him.

I take a breath and exhale slowly. The static in the room remains electrifying. I stand behind the counter absorbing what just happened and what might happen later tonight until I get distracted by what's in my hand.

He forgot his books!

Picking the first book up again, I rescan the barcode to return the book back into the library system. Repeating the process with the second and third, I pause when I get a glimpse of the fourth book, a reprint on political philosophy originally published in 1651 by Thomas Hobbes, entitled *Leviathan*.

I'm curious as to why Levi would choose such a book and I figure it's either related to his studies or because the title curiously resembles his name. I also wonder if Levi knows the term *Leviathan* is an ancient name for a sea demon.

4

ATHENA

"Bye," Levi waves as he rolls away.

There was no kiss but I'm fine with that.

I'm twirling. I had such a great time.

As I hike up the metal staircase to my studio apartment that sits above a small bakery below, I'm recollecting all of the events of the night.

Levi was such a gentleman. He opened doors for me, pulled out my chair, and he even helped me to scoot closer towards the table before he sat down to have dinner with me at the small Italian bistro down the road.

As we strolled through town he'd listened intently to my every description of the town from its history to the architecture to the folklore and the little-known secrets (some of which I probably should not have divulged like the time Henry was abducted right out of prison and right from under the sheriff's nose, although I didn't name names).

When Levi dropped me off in his Corvette convertible, I was sad to learn the car was only a rental—proof Levi was not going to stay in town for long. But he did ask to take me out again tomorrow. I feel like a fairy as I fly up the staircase in the short, mint-green sleeveless dress with a chiffon skirt that floats behind me.

I dig in my purse for my keys and... oh, shoot! I adjust my glasses as I rummage through the silver beaded clutch. I don't have my keys!

I spin around looking over the rail of the staircase to the empty bakery parking lot below. Levi is long gone.

I wiggle the doorknob to my apartment and sure enough, it's locked. I scratch my head before I turn towards the direction of the library. I can see the top of the building from here. As I take one step then another down the staircase, I figure it will only be a short walk. I do it every day and although my senses feel heightened due to the late hour—probably after 1 a.m.—I figure I have no choice because I have an extra key to my apartment there. Of course, I'll have to break into the building, but I've already done that once before, slipping through the basement window, and it'll be easier this time around.

My silver ballet flats hit the asphalt at the bottom of the staircase and I notice a faint shadow at my feet—*my* shadow. Looking up into the night sky, I see the moon is glowing, beautiful and full.

Heading towards the sidewalk, I admire the street lamps. The town association has done a fairly good job at preserving the original Victorian feel after recently installing burnished antique copper light posts that zig-zag down Main Street. But the lights, themselves, are solar and the light is already beginning to dim. Soon, the street lights will have no glow. On any normal night, I wouldn't be able to see past ten feet in front of me. So, I'm thankful for the moon brightening my path this evening.

The streets are empty. The night still feels magical but the air is stagnant until a chilly breeze blows past me.

I hear a caw. A crow perhaps? And a dark shadow feels like it's looming.

I look up. Clouds are rolling in to hide the moon.

Seeing the path ahead, a shadow unfolds like a blanket completely covering Main Street.

Hastily, I cross into the darkened street when I stop. Right in the middle there is a *tapping* noise coming from the direction where I need to go. I can't make out exactly what the tapping is though.

Is it an animal? A person? Someone's watch on their wrist ticking? Or is it their footsteps?

I recall I was not supposed to be out at night. The town is on curfew per the sheriff's orders because of the missing girls.

The tapping continues and then there is another kind of sound, except this time, it's coming from behind me.

I spin around. "Hello?" I call out but no one answers. Only a soft echo returns my words from between a dark empty alleyway.

A knocking—*is it a knocking?*—begins in addition to the tapping and I'm wondering, *what the hell is going on!*

The taps are getting louder and the knocking is turning into somewhat of a boom on repeat. Now I'm wondering if someone left their stereo on inside one of the little shops that line Main Street.

I take a step forward, but I stop again when I hear tinkering. A high pitched *tink-tink-tink* repeats itself as someone seems to be fiddling with metal.

I take a step forward, but I stop again. My heels feel damp and a cooling sensation slowly makes its way from my ankles to my shins and then above my knees. When I look down, I see my legs have disappeared up to my thighs into a thick layer of fog.

The fog is rolling. Rolling and rising. The fog behaves as

if it's breathing. The cloud is so dense, I wiggle my toes that are going numb, to make sure they are still there as I cannot see the lower portion of my legs.

I look to the library in the distance. The fog fills the street now, moving between the dated buildings as if the fog was a gathering of ghosts in search of victims.

My blood is racing. I can feel the calamity of my heart pounding in my head, which is competing with the *tap*, *knock*, and *tinker* that is getting louder and louder around me.

Where are these sounds coming from?

I feel like I'm in a dream and I wonder if perhaps I got food poisoning at dinner and am getting sick.

The fog rolls in even thicker, rising to my chest until it's over my head, so I can no longer see anything but clouds. I feel like I'm suffocating even though I can breathe. But then I sense someone come around from behind.

"Who's there?"

I'm blinking, trying to get a good look. I'm freaking out, trying to keep it together. But I figure right now would just be a good time to run from this madness!

I shuffle one foot forward when my name sounds out. "Athena."

Something has spoken my name. I say *something* because it's not a voice. My name sounded out from all around me.

I gulp, listening intently. The tapping, the knocking, the tinkering have all slowed down. I bring myself to focus on the sounds when they clamor in unison once again but more loudly this time.

"Athena."

Only a slight tap—or drip, I should say, resounds now. I realize the sounds are being made by water, dripping and banging against objects in a chorus to create speech in surround sound.

I close my heated eyes. Thirty years I've been chasing this

man, this creature, or whatever he is. Thirty years I've dreamt of this, *this* very moment, the moment I would meet a magical merman—*the* merman.

My heart is still eager to engage with him and although I'm bitter that he humiliated me earlier, my voice insists on replying back. "Captain?"

"Where have you been?" The clamor makes him sound somewhat angry. The high-pitched tinker finishes each syllable with a sharp tone.

"Why are you asking?" I'd really like to know. He's never cared before.

The fog moves swiftly across my line of sight. "Last night, you said you would return to me this evening. I waited on the beach."

I clutch my purse tight in my hand. *He was waiting for me? Then why did he embarrass me today?*

"Truthfully, I always hoped you were listening, but I was never quite sure."

"I was always listening."

"Right," I chortle. "That's your job, isn't it? To watch over the seas? To pay attention to everything that connects with the ocean?"

"Ha, I wish I could laugh," he snickers. "I pay attention to nothing and to no one. Except...," he pauses, "you."

My eyes scan the dim, damp cloud that surrounds me as my heart floats up into my throat. "Me?"

"Yes, you." The sounds—his *voice*—has deepened. "You will return with your books to the beach tomorrow to finish the latest story and you will bring another to begin."

I swallow. I've already promised Levi I'd take him on a tour of some underground passageways that lead from some old homes to the docks that were was once used by pirates to shuttle goods. They're closed off to tourists but are still maintained by the historical society.

"I... I can't," I stutter.

Cold. My toes suddenly feel colder as the fog sweeps between my legs, rolling into a dense cloud before me. I'm squinting at the cloud, trying to get a good visual as it becomes transfixed into a dense ball of rising water and the next thing I know I'm looking at a block of ice that morphs into a man. A very tall, a very brawny, a very angry-looking man. Not a merman. A man. Made of ice.

"And why not?" his glass lips are unmoved as the surround speaker of water clamoring around me speaks for him in a low tone.

He walks closer and my eyes are ogling his magnificence. *I can't believe it!* He steps with sloshy crushing sounds—ice against the pavement, which makes me feel uneasy. When he stops in front of me, I have to tilt my head back, *way* back, to look up and observe his face. His eyes are the only part that is left of his human state, encased in two perfectly fitting craters of ice, and they are fixed on me. I don't recall ever drawing his eyes this way. He doesn't look happy.

"I have a date." The words tumble out of my mouth.

Ice against ice makes more grinding noises as Willis moves his arms and legs—pacing back and forth in front of me.

"A date?" he asks.

I forgot. He likely did not use such a term in the time before he was transformed. "I mean a guy is taking me out."

"You have a gentleman who's called upon you to court you?" He clarifies, stopping in his tracks and my heart stops, too.

What am I saying? What am I telling him? I've waited forever for this—to meet Willis—and here he is in front of me! I have so many questions. So many things I also want to say.

I step closer, clutching his arm and *it burns!* "Ah!" I quickly retract.

"Don't touch, Athena!" The bang and boom of his clamoring voice vibrates into my bones and echoes as if we were in a canyon. "In this state, I will hurt you. You can never touch me like this. Just as fire burns, ice this cold causes instant decay."

Fanning my hand, I blow on my fingers, attempting to ease the pain. I see that Willis is watching me. Through odd angles of ice plus the reflection of moonlight against the edges of his glimmering frame, I think I can see what he would look like as a real man with flesh. His square jaw hosts prominent square teeth under natural plump pouty lips and a heavily curled cupid's bow. His high cheekbones sit opposite a straight long nose under a strong brow. Despite the searing throbs where my fingerprints have been removed, I would still like to touch him, touch his face. The ice is thick but looks so clear, so empty. I'd even risk kissing him to break his curse, as kisses often do in fairy tales. That giddy teenage girl who all too often fantasized about a magical merman emerges and I step closer with a pucker.

Willis steps back. He is suspicious of my intentions. I can see it in his narrowed brows. "Bad girl. You never learn."

What did I do? I'm just trying to help him.

Pieces of him break off to form smaller chunks of ice as those pieces further break off to form even smaller pieces.

"Wait!" *He's leaving! No!*

I reach out.

Before my fingers have a chance to graze against his frigid sculpture, he *explodes* into thousands of small shards of ice, which quickly materialize into little clouds.

"Willis?" I call out as the clouds gather to form a fog once again, unfolding from the center of the street—*departing*—to reveal an empty low-lit damp road illuminated by nothing but moonlight and silence.

5

ATHENA

The ocean folds over my toes. It isn't cold. It isn't warm. The temperature is just right. Laying up from dry sand, I look about. This is the most perfect beach I've ever seen. The coast stretches for miles in both directions and there is not a soul in sight. As ocean water gently folds over my toes again and again in small waves, teasing me to come swim and play, I smile to myself...

I'm in a dream.

I decide to let my mind wander and instead of getting up, I lay back flat, closing my eyes and enjoying the sun casting its warm glow over my naked body.

After another wave pools about my ankles, I feel a drip at my shin and then another at the opposite knee. More drips follow up my thigh to my center, to my belly, and finally over my breasts where each trickle becomes a welcoming tickle at my nipples that scrolls down my small pillow mounds, soothing my entire body.

I open my eyes and hovering above me is a man but not really a man. He is made of water. His features seem strong though I can't really tell what he looks like. I reach up to touch him, to run my fingers across his front, but regretfully my fingers poke right into his mass of fluidity.

It breaks my heart and I swirl my hand inside of him exactly where his heart should go when I see something—a tiny red bubble. Gently, I poke at the little blob and it pops, spreading streaks of more red bubbles.

Quickly, the streaks elongate as they also begin to twist and swirl. Faster and thicker the red streaks grow, becoming entangled upon themselves, weaving into a mass—a firm deep-red mass of muscle bigger than the size of my fist.

It beats.

My own heart thrums with what I am seeing—Willis's heart is beating. I look to his face in hopes more pieces of him will become flesh but only the orbits of his eyes besides water remains. A droplet falls onto my forehead and then another and another. I close my lids as water begins to pour, filling my every orifice, drowning my face. I gasp to breathe and slap the water—*pound* at it—only to feel more water fall...

Pounding. It's reminiscent of heavy water being thrust against a barrel in the street, which I remember from last night, but this pounding has less defined rhythm. I open my dry eyes.

And now?

I hear yelling.

"Athena!" It's the sheriff. He pounds again—harder this time.

"I'm coming," I yell, wiping the sleep from my eyes and reaching over to grab my pink and red cherry blossom printed silk robe.

Securing the robe with a tie and putting on my glasses, I open the door, squinting.

It's so bright, I must've slept in. "What can I do for you, sheriff?"

"You got those signs?"

Shoot! I forgot. "No, can I get them to you tomorrow? I'm sorry I completely—"

Pike pounds his fists on the doorframe, and then pushes his gold-framed aviator sunglasses down his nose, showing me his beady, evil, angry eyes. "Forgot?"

Oh, he seems pissed.

"Athena," he growls, "I got another missing girl reported this morning and you're telling me you forgot?"

"Sheesh, I'm sorry," I shrug.

The sheriff rests his hand on his gun. "I need those signs and I needed them up since yesterday, so get ready and head over to the library—"

"Library?" I interject. "But its Sunday. The library is closed. It's my day off and—"

"Athena! Did you not just hear what I said? Missing. *Guuuuurls.*" His eyes are about to shoot flames. "What the hell is going on with you? You were eager to help out that baby dolphin but you seem reluctant to help me with *this*. We're talking about teenagers. Young women who might be in a lot of trouble right now or worse—*dead*. I have no choice but to assume these young people have been snatched up against their will and you're worrying about library hours?"

I massage my forehead. Pike is right. I don't know what I'm thinking...

You were thinking about Willis's beating heart.

"I'm sorry, I'll get ready and head over."

"That's more like it," he says. "I'll come by the library in an hour to pick the signs up."

An hour. That's how long it takes me to get ready, walk over to the library, and draft the flyers warning folks to stay indoors after dusk due to curfew. Laying the first draft over the glass of the copy machine, I hear a knock.

"We're closed," I yell.

"But the door is open," sounds a hefty familiar voice. "You're not already trying to avoid me, are you? I thought we had a good time last night." My heart leaps as I turn to see Levi poking his head through the library's heavy front doors. "At least, *I* had a good time. Did you?" he asks bashfully, walking in cautiously with a drink in his hand. He sucks up some red liquid out of a Styrofoam cup through a clear straw.

"I did," I blush.

"Cool." He smiles, removing his glasses to place them on the checkout counter along with his drink.

He took those off on purpose. I told him how cute he was over dinner when we both took our glasses off at the same time as a dare.

"So..." He does that double snap to fist-palm thing. "I was

strolling through town looking for someplace to eat and I couldn't help but see your door was open."

"Oh, sure," I tease. "Don't lie. I know a stalker when I see one."

"Does it bother you that I'm stalking you right now? Because if it does..." Levi bites his lip, blinking puppy dog eyes at me. *He's so cute!*

"It doesn't bother me."

"Great." Levi tilts his head with curiosity. "Whatcha doin' there?"

"I'm making flyers for the sheriff."

Levi leans in closer over the counter with curiosity. "Flyers for what?"

"The sheriff is implementing a curfew on account of some missing teens. No one's allowed out after dark."

"Oh yeah? Missing teens, huh? That sounds very sad. Want me to come back there and give you a hand?"

"Um, sh-sure," I slur, trying not to drool.

You can totally come back here and give me your hand. And your lips. And your twenty-three-year-old body.

Instead of walking around, Levi takes a quick sip of his drink, places it down, and lifts his butt onto the counter, swings his legs over, and plops himself right in front of me. "How many copies are we making?"

"Two hundred," grunts an intruder. *Pike*.

"Hi, Sheriff," I turn, smiling, but it's a wasted show of teeth. As Pike smoothly struts in, his attention is fixed on the out-of-towner.

"Who are you?" Pike asks Levi directly.

Levi clears his throat, picks up and puts on his glasses, and then puts his hand out invitingly over the counter. "I'm Levi."

Pike stares at Levi's hand and instead of reaching back for a friendly shake, the sheriff places his hands at his hips, purposefully tapping his fingers across the handle of his gun. "So, let me guess." Pike tilts his head. "You're another one of these—"

"Oh no!" I shout, shaking my head and waving my hands wildly. "Levi is from the inland "He's absolutely *normal*. A *normal* human being." I'm singing at the top of my lungs in hopes the sheriff will get the picture. "Levi wears pants one hundred percent of the time." *Because he's not half fish,* I want to add.

The sheriff crinkles his nose. "Mmm. Well, I just came to make sure you weren't having any trouble getting those flyers made, Athena." The sheriff eyes the out-of-towner one more time. "You're not in any trouble, are you?"

I shake my head again. "No, I'm fine, thank you. Levi's from the university." I'm still assuming, of course.

Pike swipes his upper teeth with the front of his tongue as he studies Levi. "You look a little old to still be in college."

Levi scratches the back of his scalp seemingly flustered. "Uh... I'm..."

"He's working on his master's degree," I cut in with a lie but could totally be true. "And if you don't mind, Sheriff, Levi and I were about to engage in a debate on the mythology of the town. So, if you want to come back..."

"Come back? Sure," Pike huffs. "I get the message, Athena. I'll be back. Just don't get distracted by Mr. Harry Potter. I know how you are when it comes to discussing hocus pocus. We all know how much you love magic."

Levi squints at me with a quirk of his lips. I know I'm blushing—my face is so hot from the embarrassment, but I'm thankful at least the sheriff has offered to go away, at least for a little while.

"Jeez," Levi exhales as the door shuts behind Pike. "That guy is intense."

"I know," I reply, heading back over to the copy machine. "But he's just doing his job."

Levi picks up his drink to take a swig and follows right behind me, lifting my hair from the side of my face to plant his chin over my shoulder. "So, I was thinking you and I should go out again tonight."

Levi's breath blows warm in my ear and it makes my body hot, but strangely, I'm reminded of cold. Ice so cold it burned my fingertips and I shuffle my fingers feeling the pain.

I believe Willis will be expecting me tonight, but I'm not so sure I want to visit him anymore. Even though I know Willis *might* listen this time, I'm sure he'll still leave me to sit by myself—*alone*—in the same way he left me last night.

"Sure," I reply. "I'd love to go out again."

"Great," says Levi and he surprisingly snakes his hand around my waist. It makes me want to fan myself—I'm an inferno of hot longing. Levi places his body flush against my back. "Now, let me help you with that."

Levi lifts the lid of the copy machine with his drink still in his hand and the cup falls. *Shit!* Red soda splashes all over the machine and pools over the glass before it drips into the seams of the pane and between plastic buttons and miscellaneous cracks.

Hurriedly, I pull Levi's hand off of me and run to a janitor's closet to pull out a jumbo roll of paper towels, but by the time I get back, it's obvious the damage is done. I'm sure Levi intended to help, but instead of wiping the soda away from the top of the machine, he's opened the front panel, allowing more soda to drip into the center of the machine and over the motherboard. Despite the cord I see still plugged into the wall, the green power light is no longer lit. I'm confident we've broken the machine. I sigh as I start to clean up the mess.

"I'm sorry," says Levi, unrolling some paper towels to sop up the soda with me. "Looks like it might be broke."

"It's okay." I smile.

"So, what will you do now?"

"I'll have to make the signs by hand, I guess. I don't think the sheriff is going to be pleased."

A phone rings. Levi reaches behind him to pull his phone from his back pocket and stands up. "I have to take this," he says. "I'll be right back."

I don't mean to be nosy, but I remain quiet, listening, as I soak up more soda from the machine and then get on my knees to pat the carpet. I can't understand a word Levi is saying. He's wandered away passed three aisles of books and he's speaking so quietly, it sounds as if he's whispering.

I get up to look around. There's not a soul in here and I figure he's keeping his voice soft and low out of habit. This *is* a library.

Emerging from the aisle, Levi appears upset. "I'm sorry, I have to go."

"Oh?" *No! Please don't.*

"Yeah, a friend of mine says he needs help with one of his pets of all things. He says it's an emergency." Levi grabs more paper towels. "Here, let me help you clean this up real quick first."

"No, please," I beg. "It's fine. I got this."

"Are you sure?"

"Yeah," I nod. "What kind of pet is it?"

"A feline," he replies. "He has several."

"So, does that mean you know a lot about animals?"

"I guess you could say that," he chortles. "I was raised on a ranch. We had a lot of cats, though I know a lot more about roping cattle."

Surprising. "So, what brought you here to the coast?"

Levi's phone dings and he glances at it before he looks

back at me. "Athena, I'm really sorry. I have to go, but I'll pick you up tonight. Okay?" He skips towards the front doors.

"Sure," I smile with genuine delight, watching him leave.

My smile turns into a frown when I realize I'm going to have to call the sheriff and let him know there will yet again be another delay with these signs.

6

ATHENA

I hate this. A hundred flyers I have to write out by hand. And you would think I could just write something simple in big bold letters with a flat black sharpie, but *noooooo*.

Sadly, that is against the town's rules. Even in an emergency, they will not bend the rules. We have a law which dictates everything about posted signs, including the type of font and colors to use. The law is to protect the historic appeal of the town since the town's economy relies on tourism next to fishing.

My hand hurts and I'm hungry, so I decide to take a break. Packing up the pens and paper, I lock up the library and head back to my apartment.

Opening my refrigerator, I see there is nothing inside. I don't know why I thought there would be. I never buy groceries.

I head over to the Fiddler's Café but it's Sunday, so although I get my sandwich quickly, there's no seat available with all the tourists and students in town for the weekend. Sightings of strange creatures have been reported in waters along the coastline, and I figure with the added word of these missing girls, out-of-towners are even more curious, flocking in to catch a glimpse of *Stranger Things*. Naturally, I head back to my apartment with my turkey Reuben and jump in my car, then head towards the beach.

Once parked, I stay seated inside, unsure of whether I want to get out or not. People are present. Children are splashing, teenagers are sunbathing, tourists are ogling with their binoculars, an old man is swinging his metal detector across the sand in search of lost treasure.

I sigh.

Not one of these people knows what lurks in the ocean in front of them and not one of them would believe me if I told them. I decide I need to be more like these people—carefree and not so much a crazy person. I shouldn't worry about Willis. Every encounter we've had, he quickly disappeared. If I show no interest, I'm sure he'll leave me alone.

As he always has.

Getting out, I grab my sandwich and bag, and then my blanket and umbrella from the trunk. Walking my flip-flop covered feet several yards through hot sand, I find a smooth sunny spot near the water where I set up shop and get busy stuffing my face of turkey on a huge hoagie and creating more flyers.

Within hours, I'm spent and I lay my head down on the blanket when I spy families packing up to leave. They are all leaving, apart from a young couple running around on the beach. The couple looks to be in their late teens or early twenties. The tall, lean young man chases the curvy brunette of bronzed skin up and down the peaks of small sand hills until he captures her, throwing her to the ground to topple over her and kiss her. She throws sand in his face and he picks her up with a devious smile to walk her into the water where he laughs and she screams as he tosses her into the ocean. She makes a splash before she emerges, wrapped in a glistening wet warm glow made amber from the setting sun. She kisses him. They wrap their arms around each other, kissing with more depth, swapping copious amounts of spit, and I wonder what it must be like to be caught in a kiss like that. The moment seems enchanting. They look like something right out of a fairy tale or *worse*, a cheesy teen chick flick from the eighties. They're so cute. *I hate them.*

I squeal with a tight pinch to my toe and quickly turn around, kicking my foot at the source of my pain—*a crab?*

"Damn you!" I curse as the thing the size of my palm stares at me, pokes its weird antennae eyes at me, and shows off its pincher with a squeezing action.

"Shoo." I kick at the crustacean, which doesn't move.

Removing my flip-flop, I flick at it, nearly whacking the crab, and watching the animal finally scurry towards the waterline. A tiny wave rolls over the crustacean, swallowing it, and I feel guilty that might be the end of the small creature. I may have sentenced it to death. I wait, hoping to see the crab emerge from the water when suddenly, I feel alone.

Searching for the kissing couple, I see they are gone. Turning my head about, I realize I *am* alone. There isn't a soul in sight. Night's blanket is creeping its way across the heavens as the sun has already sunken below the horizon. A few stars twinkle through the black-to-blue gradient above me and as I shove my pens back into my bag, I read one of the signs I've been working on: Public Notice. Curfew in Effect After Dusk. Strictly Enforced by Order of the Sheriff.

I remember the reasons I've been working on these signs and I shudder with the thought I could become one of them —the *missing*. I wonder what's happened to them. Three. Missing. Girls. Surely, nothing good.

Hurriedly, I fold up my blanket and bend down under the umbrella to grasp the latch that will bring the umbrella fabric to a close when something quickly crawls across the top of my foot.

Frantically, I squeal, kicking and falling to my butt when I see that stinking crab. It's eyeballing me again. Trying to freak me out.

"If you keep up with this, I'm going to put you in a kettle and boil you," I snap. The crab clamps its pinchers at me again, taunting me, so I take a leap towards the crustacean ready to chase it, but I stop.

This is insane. I'm playing with a dumb beach crab and I need to get off the beach and get indoors before I get nabbed. By what? Who knows? But I need to pack up and head home.

Turning around, I feel a painful nip at the tendon above my heel. *Damn this crustacean won't leave me alone!* I reach down to trap the critter with both hands, but it escapes me, heading once again towards the water. This time, however, the crab stops right before it reaches the edge of a wave fanning across the sand and my breath hitches at the sight of a red rowboat, which seems to have come out of nowhere.

The boat, made of wood, looks old. A few barnacles surround the front end. Slowly, the boat, made to hold maybe two people at most, rocks slightly as small waves push the front end to become wedged into the sand onshore.

I adjust my glasses, searching the water for any sign of him—*Willis*.

I know it's him, though I don't know exactly what I'm expecting to see. He is, after all, comprised of the very thing in front of me—the ocean. I suspect he would like me to get into the boat, but I'm reluctant to climb in. He's never presented me with such an offer before. Many times, he's turned me away—tipping me over before I can get beyond hip deep from shore.

And there's no paddle. *What does he expect me to do? Trust him? After he sprayed me in front of the others and left me with burnt fingers?*

I turn my back to the ocean. Cora Morae once warned me to never do such a thing.

"The ocean is unpredictable," she said. "It is as tempestuous as the atmosphere and has as much transgression as the beasts that live within its depths."

I never realized until now Ms. Morae was, in actuality, referring to Willis and the other mermen, or perhaps their tempers.

A spray of water hits me from behind and my shirt is soaked once again at the back.

"Stop doing that!" I snap with a turn to face Willis, expecting to see some resemblance of a man, but there is nothing. Only the swell of another wave rolls in and crashes with a fan across the sand.

I huff and cross my arms. I don't understand why he behaves so mysteriously although I guess I can't blame him for not communicating. He can't exactly speak whenever he wishes...

Wait...

What's this?

As the wave rolls back into the sea, I must admit I am tickled. I clasp my hands to my mouth to hide my smile when I see words written in cursive in the sand.

It reads: ***How else may I get your attention?***

I skip to the words and rub my toes across the beautifully scripted cursive letters on the beach, but I pause when I realize I'm wet yet again. "I don't like being sprayed," I respond.

Another wave fans, moving further inland to curl about my feet. As the water flows away, a new message appears: ***Get in the boat.***

I scrub my heel against the beach, scribbling over his words. "No."

More water rushes over his words to be replaced by new words. ***Why not?***

"I don't trust you."

You've been following me through the length of your existence and now, you don't trust me?

"You're crueler than I thought you were."

Cruel? How have I been cruel?

"My whole life you hid from me. People believed I was crazy though I never faltered in my belief you existed. You've repeatedly abandoned me and when we finally came face to face, you embarrassed me."

A wave rolls, but it does not come up on shore. A breeze blows and my skin chills. Rubbing my arms, I look up to see more stars are twinkling.

Water pools at my feet and flows away. ***I won't play with you like that again***, he writes.

"Play? Is that what you thought you were doing? Do you think it's okay to play with people like that? I don't like to be played with."

No, I suppose not. You're no longer the child I saved. You're a woman now.

What did he say? "You saved me?"

Yes, against my better judgment, I intervened.

He saved me! This is why I've been obsessed with him. I always knew we were connected, but the trailing comment undeniably hurts. "Against your better judgment? Are you saying you wished you hadn't saved me? Left me to die?"

I'm saying I wished I'd done a better job of not letting myself be known to you.

Odd. "Why?"

Because you've spent your entire life chasing mermen.

"There's nothing wrong with that," I confess. "I've loved

LOVERS IN DEEP

doing the research. I've fallen in love with the folklore. I enjoy knowing I'm an expert—an expert in magic. I'm confident there are many folks who would give up all their real-world possessions to know the things I do."

But you deserve more than magic**, Athena. **You deserve love. Real love.

I don't understand what is going on here. It seems he wants me to give up my chase on magic and mermen, but he wants me to get into the boat. Of course, I'm suddenly afraid to go. I've never feared to be in Willis's presence before, but this is the first time I've ever gotten an invite, which makes me suspicious. Still, there is an undeniable ache to get to know more about him. I figure it's the scholar in me and I march my feet towards the paddleless rowboat and get in. "Where are you taking me?" I look at the sand.

To a place known only to me. That's what you want isn't it, Athena? To learn more about me?

"Yes," I admit although I have to say I've dreamt of more. *Much* more. *Physical* more. *Intimate* more. Even though I don't really know him.

We must travel across this great sea, he writes. ***The journey will last several hours. Are you sure you'd like to go? Do you trust me?***

I smile, getting comfortable. "I've always trusted you before, Willis. It's you who never trusted me."

Water flows in gentle waves to surround the boat and I am lifted and then pushed towards the darkening open sea.

For the first few hours, the journey is lovely. Stars shine brighter than I have ever known them to be. And there are so many of them! Like an intricately woven web, stars sprawl to sparkle across the night sky. Millions of stars I'd never seen before twinkle and I get the feeling they aren't just twinkling but winking at me.

I spy Orion and the bull, Taurus, my favorite constellations. I regret Theseus, the greatest and my most favorite hero in Greek mythology, is not among the stars. "Perhaps," I tell Willis, "There is more to Theseus' story that has yet to be written, which is why he is not up there. What do you think?" I ask, but recall that Willis cannot reply.

Though I know I am in his company, it still feels lonely out here and I wonder how Willis feels about living where he does—without genuine human contact and virtually living in the middle of nowhere. The worst is it's boring.

I hunker down to lay curled on my side. My lids are getting heavy. As I shut my eyes, Willis continues to swiftly push the boat across the ocean's surface adding a gentle tip from side to side, and I smile to myself. He's rocking me to sleep.

Shuffling and a soft screech. The sounds funnel through my ears and I open my eyes.

Wood. I'm surrounded by chipped and moldy wood painted red under an awakening blue sky. I remember I fell asleep in a rowboat made for two, although I had to sleep alone so Willis could push me.

Shuffling and more screeching ensues. Someone or some*thing* sounds like it's trying to get into the boat and I sense I'm no longer moving.

I pop my head up over the edge when my ears are overtaken by an influx of cries and shrieks. I shriek myself but am quickly silenced as sand is thrown into my face.

"Monkeys?" I snort... and blink... and spit. "Yuck." Sand has found its way into facial crevices I had no idea I had.

Hastily, the fur-covered critters scurry across the beach towards the edge of a tropical forest line, but they keep their heads poked out of the foliage to assess me. They don't look dangerous but then again, there are at least thirty or forty of them and they all appear to have very large white square front upper incisors laid between very long, sharp yellowing fangs. They could easily attack me. Adrenaline surges. I think I've gone into *fight or flight* mode.

"Willis?" I call out and a wave unfolds, knocking the boat.

Peeping over the edge, I see he's left an arrow in the sand. It points straight towards the edge of the forest line, through the line of gawking monkeys.

"You want me to go that way? I don't think so." I shake my head. "Where are we?"

Another wave fans across the beach to reveal the arrow once again and the word, **Home**.

I take a breath and get up. I remember I've been waiting for this. I didn't just want to prove the existence of mermen but I'd secretly hoped Willis would find some connection with me to whisk me away to his fantasy island and *whaddya know?*

Here I am.

He and I—we *are* connected, and I'm about to plant my feet on Fantasy Island. But like a dummy, I'm hesitating.

Another wave knocks the front end.

"All right," I grumble.

Stepping out of the boat, I lick my lips. My mouth is so dry.

My feet get wet before more words appear at my feet. ***Thirsty? Cup your hands.***

Cup my hands? I do as Willis asks and to my delight, water fills my palms. I take a drink. The water tastes as crisp and clean as if it had been purified through reverse osmosis. I cup my hands again, watching them fill up, realizing he's able to do this. Willis controls water. That is his power. He's pulling unseen droplets from the atmosphere and allowing it to collect in my palms.

Feeling refreshed, I spy the monkeys spying me back. "Are you sure those animals are not going to hurt me?"

They're my friends.

I step on the 'F' and walk up the beach. "Of course, you have friends that are monkeys. You're a sea captain. If you were human, you would have one of those critters dressed in a pirate's coat and sitting on your shoulder."

My butt gets sprayed from behind and I'm furious! I told him I don't like that, although apparently, the monkeys do. Shrieks and shrills erupt in a chorus of what I assume is laughter accompanied by applause. *The monkeys are laughing at me.* I don't know why I should feel humiliated in the presence of simians. One of them—a baby in his mother's lap—is bouncing with such delight, it makes me chuckle a little and I decide to make my way into the forest while they're amused.

I head straight towards where Willis's arrow was pointing. Pushing through a few oversized leaves, I find a path made of flat, foot-sized black stones and I can imagine Willis somehow laid this path for himself to walk upon when he was in his solid icy form. The stones are smooth under my feet, making for an easy hike.

There is a bit of an incline and I pause to take a breather. My stomach growls, which is embarrassing and I look around, wondering if Willis is close, but I don't see him anywhere.

I squeal when a little monkey plops on my head, his tiny fingers gripping my hair, but I calm myself when he hands me an unusually small banana.

"Thank you," I say, taking the banana and peeling the fruit open. It's so small, barely bigger than my thumb, so I pop the whole thing in my mouth and gulp it down with one swallow.

As I skip onward along the path taking in the sweet scent of tropical flowers, the monkey stays with me on my head with his soft fuzzy tail wrapped around my neck. He mumbles—random squeaks mixed with puffs—and although I tell him I can't understand what he's saying, he continues to tell his story in monkey talk.

Ahead, I see the path is about to end. Ferns and palm trees open to a clearing and I'm fascinated with what I see. The stones lead straight into a small pool at the edge of a steep cliff made of black rock.

I stick a foot into the clear water with a glimmering bottom. It's shallow. The water barely covers my ankles, so I put both feet in, feeling tiny pebbles massage under the bare soles of my feet. Trinkets also appear to sparkle between pebbles and I bend down to take a closer look.

The monkey on my head shrieks and points at what I believe is a piece of gold. Reaching in to pull out the treasure, the monkey snatches the coin from me and scurries away. *Little thief!* I pull out another coin to examine it. This coin, a doubloon, looks exactly like Henry's, which Shelley wears around her neck.

Sifting through more stones, I find more coins and even a gem. Lifting what appears to be a ruby to the sky, I peer through the red stone to examine the kaleidoscope of light. *What people would pay for this*, I wonder. The jewel reminds me of my dream—the one I'd had of Willis's heart—and I toss the stone back into the pool.

This is sad, really. This is the place Willis calls home, but there's nothing among all this treasure that gives any further clues as to who he is other than a collector. And it's all hidden. Like Willis's soul, there's nothing here but lost treasure.

Raking my hands through stones and coins and gems, I'm caught off guard by a stick of plastic, which doesn't belong. I lift it up—it's my pen! I lost this pen years ago on the beach.

Eyes open in the water, glaring. It's a bit strange, but I know it's him and my cheeks warm. "You saved my pen." I smile, clutching the pen to my chest.

Knowing Willis is with me reminds me that I'm parched and I cup my hand in the pool to take a drink, but the water drains from my palm. I cup the water again, only to watch the water slip between my fingers.

I scowl at the eyes beneath me. "I'm thirsty."

Willis's eyes roll to look above me. I look up as well to spy what he's looking at when I see water is springing from the top of the cliff. I stand up, tossing my glasses to a grassy patch, and readying myself to get wet as I stick out my tongue.

Water showers over my face—gently at first, but my body comes alive with a heavier pour. I take a few gulps before I'm turning around to feel the massage of a cool cleanse washing all the saltiness that had stuck to my skin and made my hair stiff and coarse. I lift off my dress to rinse and wring it out, feeling refreshed and clean.

Tossing my dress to a boulder on the wing, I let my hands rub over my body before I splash and spin to dance in the waterfall. But I stop when the temperature changes. The water gets cold and I know I'm being watched. I'd almost forgotten I wasn't alone. Turning my back to the cliff, my breath hitches with the sight of the iceman standing on the stone path before me, watching me.

"Come," I say, reaching out my hand.

He shakes his head.

"We don't have to touch. Just join me."

He shakes his head again.

I bow my chin. I'm so frustrated. It feels like I've been carrying this obsession with this man around in my mind forever and I finally know why—because he saved me.

Somewhere in my subconscious, I've figured I owe him and now I'm desperate, more desperate than ever to save him back.

"There's got to be a way, Willis. Tell me what it is. Whatever you need to put you back in your human form, I'll gladly give it to you. Whatever price needs to be paid, I will—"

The water flowing over my back turns icy as Willis, himself, bursts into a thousand shards of ice. The ice falls to the ground in the shape of an arrow pointing back down the path.

Perhaps I've said too much or overstayed my welcome.

"I don't want to leave." I hug myself, trying to withstand the freezing downpour pummeling over my back.

My feet get uncomfortably cold and I fear I have no choice but to step out of the pool before they become numb and I'm unable to walk.

Treading across the pebbles, I come onto the path. My hands are trembling—I'm freezing! Reaching for my glasses and dress, I find that it's all dry and I'm thankful that Willis has removed every water molecule from the fabric.

Slipping my dress over my head, a cool splash folds about my ankles. Looking down, I see pieces of treasure that have been laid at my feet. I figure Willis wants me to take these coins and gems, including a pearl necklace and a tiara with a few missing diamonds. He's giving them to me. I believe this is really the reason he brought me here—to pay me off. But for what? It doesn't matter. I don't want any of it.

"I already have the treasure I want, Willis. I have knowledge of you and as soon as you lay with me, you will be a man again. I know you're afraid you might hurt me, or perhaps even kill me, but nothing would make my life more complete than to see you walk. You can have my body. I will gladly give it to you. It's the least I can do since you not only saved my life but filled it with such wonderful mystery and magic. I've had the most mystical existence. You deserve to be a man again, so you can enjoy the rest of yours."

I wait for a response but, as usual, he doesn't do anything. The arrow made of crushed ice remains fixed, pointing back down the path.

My teeth chatter. I'm still a little cold and after a few monkeys poke their heads out of the brush to spy sadly at me, I decide to head back to the boat.

7
WILLIS

Swiftly, I push Athena across the ocean's surface back to her town. The voyage takes several hours and although the wind in her hair makes her smile, it's obvious she's annoyed with me. I've offered her all I can give—the finest treasures I've collected for the last few centuries, but I should've known such things would not appeal to her.

And why did I want her to have those things?
I'm not sure.

But the fact she's denied such fine treasures upsets me. She is unlike other women. She's stubborn, as stubborn as she was when she was a child. The urge to tip her over and swat her behind with a lash of my belt...

Aye, the urge is overwhelming. Lucky for her, I have no legs and therefore, no pants. So, no need for a belt.

Pushing Athena close to shore, I watch from below the surface to see her step out. As her toes slip into the water, I regret that I've brought her back so soon.

Her heels plant in the sand causing a small flurry and I look at her legs. They have a slight pink hue. I regret that, too. I've cooked her. After traveling the seas for hours under the sun, I've allowed her skin to burn. She will be in much discomfort for days to come. The thought that I should be the one to ease her discomfort with oils soothed over her body by my hands...

Truth be told, the thought of my hands on her excites me, but I quickly toss the thought away as I have no hands to touch her with.

Athena makes her way back to her things on the beach. She shuffles through her belongings and finds her communication box. I wonder who she's communicating with and when I see her blush with a smile and a bite of her bottom lip, I am sure her reactions are the result of being wooed by her gentleman caller. Athena has yet to look back to me to say farewell or make a promise to return, as she always does. Her eyes remain fixed on the device in her palm as if she's obsessed with the box. She cannot look away from her communications, including while she is packing up her things. Within minutes, her bag is over her shoulder with an umbrella in hand and she is strolling away.

Watching her leave, I am beside myself. The woman doesn't even look back. Not even after the journey we just made together. She *always* looks back with eyes so enormously wide they speak everything of how desperate she's been to prove I exist—begging for a sign, any sign that I would show myself to her.

Though she hates it, I'm tempted to shoot water at her again to get her attention, to force her to come back even if it means she will be upset to yell at me, but I decide to keep still. I have no clue if I've upset her so much that she will no longer come to visit to talk or read to me. The idea that my existence will once again be a lonely one...

I don't understand my feelings. I can't bare the thought Athena might never return. If I had a heart, I believe it would be aching. Bleeding!

What is this? What are these? Feelings? For Athena?

Watching her disappear over the sand dune, I can only imagine where her long thin legs are headed. She's going to walk those beautiful, burnt-to-a-crisp legs to mix and mingle with another's.

Damn her and damn *her gentleman caller.*

If I had legs, *real* legs, that woman wouldn't be so eager to run away.

If I had arms, *real* arms, I'd wrap them around her and give that woman everything she'd always wished for and then some.

With *real* hands and a *real* tongue, I'd tease and prod and poke at that woman until she was cursing, giving her a real reason to run, but I would not let her go.

And if I had my body, I'd give it to her—*smother* her— teach her a lesson for always wanting so much. I'd give her every *Goddamned* fucking thing she ever wanted—me, my flesh, my bones. Because that's what she's really been after and I'd give her everything.

Every. Piece. Of. Me.

Including the piece I believe she wants most. The piece she's been saving herself for. And just when Athena thinks she's had her fill, I'd give her that piece again and again until she bursts at the seams but only on my command, hollering, "Oh, Captain! Please, Captain! Yes, Captain!" in obedience.

But, I don't have legs, hands, or a body at my disposal. I do know, however, where I can get those pieces of me back.

"Well, it's about time." Lenora folds her hair away from her face.

This is the first time I've seen Lenora's hair loose. I suspect she's freed her mane to match her newfound disposition. Since acquiring the other seamen's powers, the witch's attitude has changed. She seems more pleasant. One would think with so much magic at her disposable, she'd be wielding those powers to her advantage—wreaking havoc without mercy. But instead, she's made a new home for herself inside an old sunken pirate ship, which she's decorated rather nicely, keeping her quiet as of late. I also see she no longer keeps pets—no more prisoners in chains—like she used to.

"I should've known you'd be waiting for me," I say without actually making a sound. The power Lenora has over sea beasts, which she obtained from Orphelius, makes it easy for the sea witch to read my mind.

"Not you," Lenora chuckles, a hint of sarcasm in her tone. "I've been waiting on your *powers.*"

The witch stands, kicking the stool out from under her

arse at the Captain's table. The stool floats with a gentle tumble as she walks over to a full-length mirror to look at herself. She's fully dressed in contemporary attire. She's wearing men's trousers of modern times and a collared shirt. She tugs on the collar, attempting to lift the folds up higher on her neck, but the fold won't stay upright since we are underwater.

"What are you up to, Lenora? Have you been playing with my brothers and I all along?"

"Playing?" She twitches. "You of all people should know I don't play."

"No. You don't. You curse, which is the reason we are in this mess in the first place."

"How dare you?" She crosses her arms. "Do you think I like handing out curses? Do you think I wanted to bring this fate upon us? I'll have you know, I hate the sea. I never wanted to board that vessel centuries ago to become a slave in some unknown world. I cursed the ship to save myself and the other poor souls aboard from torture. It's not my fault you and your fellow seamen did not heed my warning. I warned you not to come back onboard, Captain."

"So, what now?" I ask because I am at Lenora's mercy and I figure if we do not come to some type of agreement, we will remain as we are and at an impasse for all eternity.

"Now," she replies, "we strike a deal."

"You want my power," I affirm, though I believe I should warn Lenora. "I'll have you know the power to control the sea is not all it's cracked up to be. Though I have the power to control the ocean's motions, I am also at its mercy. The sea has higher masters than me. The celestial bodies—the earth, sun, moon—they are all masters of the ocean that you will have to learn to obey. Not to mention, humans. They have no control over how the waves behave, but humans will stop at nothing to gain dominion over all seas, which cannot be allowed or they will destroy it. It's a great responsibility. Not for one day have I felt as though I've possessed magic. The power to control water isn't magic at all and certainly not the type of magic my Athena seeks."

"*Your* Athena." Lenora laughs. "Typical. She's not *yours*. That girl is not a *thing* to possess or *own*."

If I had teeth, I'd be gritting them right now. "You know damn well that's not what I meant."

"That's exactly what you meant!" Lenora roars. "You want to possess that girl as badly as she wants to possess you. The only difference is you're too stupid to allow yourself to be under *her* command."

Under her *command?* The thought baffles me.

"Can you imagine it, Willis?"

"Imagine what?"

"Imagine what it might be like to have a captain of your own?"

Where is the witch going with this? "I am my own Captain."

"Of course, you are. Of course, Willis, but imagine this..."

The witch floats and twirls, pointing to the mirror, and I see Athena. She's naked. If I had a heart, it would be thrumming against the cavern of my chest. I've never seen Athena looking so lovely. *Beautiful.* I scan the full length of her body. I had no idea small, perky bosoms could appeal to me so much. Her breasts are perfectly bite-sized and I imagine how they might feel completely engulfed in my mouth and the reaction her body would have as I suckled them.

Athena combs her wet hair. It appears as though she's primping herself, and I regret that she's likely adorning rouge and glossing her lips for another.

"Look at her," Lenora interrupts my thoughts. "And look at you."

Look at me? Is she kidding? If I had hands, I would break

that mirror into thousands of pieces. "I see nothing of myself. There's nothing to see but water."

"Water isn't so bad," Lenora smirks. "Athena likes you in this form. In fact, the poor woman has become an expert on your unnatural state. Though, I do think it's sad Athena has yet to navigate you. Why haven't you let her?"

This witch is a loony. "What nonsense are you speaking?"

"Think about it. Wouldn't it be grand to give that woman full reign of Captain's duties? To let her roam over you? Just think of how nice it would be to let that woman explore you, your body—a *human* body. Then, you could give Athena complete authority in handling all your precious cargo, but..." The witch laughs to herself. "If only you had flesh and *bone*."

Looking at Athena in the mirror, preparing herself, I am imagining it—myself inside of the goddess. I imagine what her pink, sunburnt skin must taste like and what her warmth must feel like. I imagine the two of us together: on the beach, in a boat, in the backseat inside of her mechanical carriage as I've observed young people parked along the beach at wee hours of the night. With Athena's legs wrapped around my waist, I imagine myself—

Lenora interrupts my imagination. "Admit that you want Athena and I'll give you legs." I stare the witch down through the mirror. "And stop looking at me like that," she scoffs. "Your eyeballs are ghastly looking without sockets to hold them. You knew before you came here, Captain, there'd be a price to pay. The question is do you love this woman enough to pay it? The price for legs is non-negotiable."

I search my soul. I'm still not quite sure I know what love is, much less what I should pay.

Lenora begins to gather her floating hair into a bun, readying to work her magic, despite the fact I have not yet agreed. "And by the way, Captain, I should tell you that if there ever were a time to reveal your true nature to Athena, that time is *now*. I've already tried to warn the woman about the demon chasing her. If she isn't able to shake herself from the demon's lure, her very essence is going to be lost. If this demon's snake should sneak its way into Athena's virgin vessel, the Athena we know—the goddess of wisdom and wishful thinking—will forever cease to exist."

With the witch's words, I realize there is no more need for negotiation. "Give me more than just flesh and bone," I tell the witch. "I want *all* of my mass back."

8

ATHENA

A hundred texts—that's how many messages I had to scroll through after I got back from my one-day trip with Willis. Never have I ever felt so important. Levi, Shelley, and the sheriff all began with messages wanting something from me but after I did not respond right away, as I always do, they seemed genuinely worried.

Of course, I called the sheriff first because I knew I was going to get an ass chewing for going MIA, especially without having any flyers ready.

Shelley, I called second to calm her anxiety. The sheriff had enlisted her help with the flyers and she was afraid I'd become one of the missing. Considering her family history, I was not surprised to get an ass-chewing from her as well.

Last, I called Levi. I'd stood him up. It took me a half hour to come up with a good reason why I couldn't keep our date or much less call him back. I told him I hadn't slept the night before after our first date because I couldn't stop thinking about him and that I'd passed out hard on a lounge chair in the library and my battery had died. Thankfully, he bought the lie I gave him and he asked me out again.

But by the time I'd gotten to Levi's call, I'd already made plans to make flyers for the sheriff with Shelley and the gang at the beach house. Levi insisted on joining in after getting me into so much trouble with the sheriff and breaking the copy machine. So, after I made one more call to Shelley, I got the okay to bring a guest. To think, I'll finally get those flyers done in plenty of good company, although I wonder what the seamen, Orphelius and Henry, will think of Levi.

Reaching for my glasses, I pause. Tonight, I decide I'm going to wear my contacts. I rarely wear them. My mother encouraged me to wear contact lenses all through high school, but I chose not to. People, or *boys*, usually left me alone as long as I was wearing my glasses. Levi seems to like to look at me with *and* without the glasses.

My pulse quickens when I think about him looking at me so hungrily again.

After placing the second lens into my eye, I blink. My vision comes into focus and I see myself in the mirror but I'm not exactly sure what I'm looking at.

Sure, I see me. I see towels hanging to the left behind me and the framed seashell art above the towel rack, but I get the strangest feeling there's something behind the mirror. There's something I should be seeing but is invisible, as if I'm being watched—from beyond.

My initial thought is of Willis and I get the strangest feeling something is not right with him. Dread washes over me. Quickly, I turn on the faucet and call out to him.

"Willis?" I don't know what I'm expecting to see.

Him? Or any resemblance of him?

But I see nothing. Only a stream of water scented with a hint of chlorine flows straight from the spout and down into the drain.

I feel so stupid. I just spoke to a faucet. I can't recall the last time I'd felt this dumb, but dumb feelings do seem to recur often with Willis. I'm completely alone and yet Willis has still found a way to humiliate me.

I reach for my mascara. It's been a long time since I've worn mascara since it doesn't matter when I wear my glasses. Not to mention, mascara and water don't get along, but I'm sure Levi will appreciate a double coat over my long lashes either way.

"You look great tonight," Levi smiles, pulling along the side of the road to park his rental Corvette in front of Shelley's beach house.

"Thanks," I smile with a quiver of my lips. I'm desperate to contain my smile from getting too big, showing how overly excited I am, like a girl rather than a woman.

I reach for the door to get out, but Levi pulls at my arm. "Hey, wait a sec."

I turn to him. He's biting his bottom lip and staring at me with those big puppy dog eyes again. He wants something.

"What's up?" I ask.

His lashes flutter as he takes off his glasses. "I was thinking maybe I could go over to your place after this and we could hang out." His finger trails my shoulder and then my collarbone.

My core ignites!

"M-m-my place?" I stutter.

"Yeah," he cocks his head, grabbing my hand to pull my fingers to his lips where he kisses them.

Oh my God, I'm on fire!

I exhale. I know exactly what he's asking and for the first time *ever*, I'm not afraid to give in. After the sensual moment under the waterfall, making me feel a deeper longing than I've ever known, Willis left me in the cold. I'd never felt so empty or needy. I need to feel warmth. I need to feel full. I want to be desired and Levi clearly desires to be with me. But I need to be the big girl here and be honest with Levi. He's twenty-three and I'm thirty. I'm sure he has plenty of experience, but I have none and I don't want to be a huge disappointment.

I pull his hand to my lap. "Levi, I have to tell you something."

"Uh-oh." He grimaces. "Am I being too forward? I'd invite you over to my place, but I don't actually have one. I'm living with a friend on a bo—"

"I'm a virgin," I cut in.

Levi's face falls flat, blood draining from his cheeks. He turns white, his jaw dropping, his eyes blinking blankly.

For heaven's sake, is it really that bad? Jeez, I thought some guys might be happy about it. "Levi?"

He leans back in the driver's seat, rocking his head back, bumping his skull gently against the headrest a few times.

Watching the rocking motion makes me feel ill. "Levi, if

you don't want to stick around, I understand. I can have one of the others take me home."

"No, no," he coos, leaning over and gripping me by that back of the head to pull me to him. He kisses my forehead and my sunken spirit is lifted. "Let's enjoy this time with your friends and decide what we want to do later. Okay?"

Despite his assurance, I'm still worried about what he thinks. He must think I'm a prude being as old as I am. "Are you sure? You seem disappointed."

He shakes his head, gripping my chin. "No, I'm not disappointed. Not at all. I knew you were something special when I met you, but now I'm sure you're worth even more."

Levi kisses my fingers again before he scoots out, flashing his pearly whites. "Let me open the door for you."

Levi comes around, takes my hand, and helps me out of the car. It's sweet and I think to myself how stupid I've behaved for the last three decades. I've been so obsessed with mermen that I've neglected to consider how a *real* man might make me feel.

And good golly me! Levi makes me feel good.

He puts his hand at my back as we walk up the front steps to the beach house. The gesture makes me think he's as happy to be with me in this moment as I am with him. We pause at the top of the landing to look at one another as cheers erupt amidst outbursts of laughter from inside the beach house. Shelley and Kumiko, along with the seamen, are already having a cheery good time.

Levi knocks on the door.

Orphelius answers, his smile beams brightly below shiny, red rosy cheeks. "Athena!" he shouts. "Come in. Oh, you are a lovely goddess. We are so happy you've decided to give up your scholarly pursuits to join us this evening." He hiccups. Or burps. One or the other. Orphelius has already had his fill of booze—*obviously*.

"We still have to make the flyers," I remind him.

The seaman's brow furrows, and his voice gets low. "Of course. Shameful business for such young people to go missing, robbed right out from under their loved ones' noses." Orphelius scans Levi from head to toe. "Don't you think, mate?"

Levi clears his throat. "Uh... yeah."

We a hear a woman shout from inside. "Orphelius, are you going to let Athena in?" I see it's Shelley, waving.

Orphelius moves to the side, opening the door. "Please come in. Have a seat at the table, why don't you?" Once I step through, Orphelius plants his hand on Levi's chest. "Not you."

"Orphelius!" I snap.

Orphelius hooks his arm around Levi's shoulders and yanks the leaner man to his side. "This young man needs a beer. He's coming with me back outside. Henry and I have been brewing our own ale in the shed we built out back. Come, lad! Let's get you drunk while the women do the lawman's busy work."

Levi seems ambivalent as he is escorted away and I debate with myself whether I should save him. But the debate quickly comes to a halt as Shelley shuts the door, separating us.

"Hey, girl." She hugs me. "Have a seat at the table. Are you hungry?"

"You must be," adds Kumiko. "I heard you had a long night last night. Took a trip and everything."

Took a trip? I'm baffled. "How do you know?"

Kumiko shrugs. "A seagull told me."

My nose crinkles. "Really?"

"Mhm." She nods.

I walk towards the table and see Henry in his wheelchair with a huge smile on his face, scribbling on paper—communicating with someone, a very *big* someone, who I don't recognize. His back is to me and *Jesus!* The guy is ripped. Rock solid. The light aqua blue T-shirt he's wearing is stretched at the seams allowing every contour of his muscly back to bulge through. And his shoulders! They are buckling as he peels an orange, no a mandarin, and I see the squirt of citrus spray as I suspect he's chomped hard into a tiny juicy wedge.

His laugh is also tremendous—low—but so husky and loud the old wooden floors of the beach house shake beneath my sandaled feet.

The man with a tan and hints of toasted pink and peach drops the mandarin peel on the table and rakes his hefty fingers through his sun-kissed shoulder length, wavy blond hair. I swallow, trying to contain the emerging gasp as I watch his deltoids and triceps tense and flex when he picks up another mandarin to peel it. By the look of the stack of peels, he's had to have eaten an entire orchard's worth.

Henry makes eye contact with me and flashes a brilliant smile, holding his hand out across from him, indicating that I sit down. Right. Next. To. The. Big. Guy.

Big guy turns around and... *Oh, dear Lord.* I feel faint. The fluttering blink of his stormy gray eyes shoots lightning, electrifying me. But the pink in his cheeks accompanied by a sweet smile embedded in a square jawline masked over with a shadow of scruff makes me woozy.

"Athena!" The big guy jerks up, knocking his chair over.

"Athena!" sounds another with a higher-pitched tone accompanied by a few stomps from behind me. Swiveling, I see Levi barging back in the front door. "Athena, you have to try this," he says, cupping my bottom and planting a glass filled to the brim with bubbly clear amber liquid topped with foam in front of my face. "These guys made this. Try it. It's homemade beer. It's amazing."

"I don't drink beer," I confess, sliding the glass out of view. I can't take my eyes off the stranger, who is beginning to look familiar, though I'm confident I've never seen him before. Not to mention, he's got to be from out of town because I keep records on everyone who lives here, including the regular tourists.

"Well, that's too bad," replies Levi, taking a swig of his ale before he kisses my forehead as he did in the car.

Although it tickled me earlier, I blush with embarrassment this time. Levi's action also seems to have caught the attention of everyone in the room and they're all staring.

Except for the big guy.

He's staring *and* gritting his teeth.

"I think you should take a sip. You need to live it up a little," Levi continues. "After what you told me in the car, Athena, it's like you've been living on a secluded island your whole life."

"And what's wrong with that?" interrupts the stranger.

"Nothing," Levi shakes his head in a quandary.

The two men eye each other up.

"I'm sorry, man. Have I offended you somehow?" asks Levi.

The big guy looks offended and I swear it seems he's about to pounce on poor Levi and really hurt him for some unknown reason.

Snaking my arm around Levi's back, I turn my head about the room as a reminder that I've brought Levi as my guest. When I make eye contact with the big guy, his face softens.

"Excuse me," says the stranger. "I don't mean to sound brash. What's your name?"

"Levi." My date responds.

"I apologize Levi. I've just recently returned from a long voyage. I've been told being away at sea has a tendency to make a man mad. Please—" the big guy picks up the furniture he knocked over, dusts off the seat, and presents it to Levi. "Have a seat in the Captain's chair."

Wait...
What did he say?
The Captain's *chair?*

9
WILLIS

*A*s Levi graciously takes a seat along with the others. While the men clear their peels and Shelley loads the table with a barge worth of pasta, salad, and bread, I see Athena doesn't move. She seems stuck. She bows her head to look at her painted toes.

"Athena," calls Shelley. "Honey, sit down."

Athena bites her lip. Her nostrils flare as she squeezes her eyes shut.

"Girl, c'mon," encourages Kumiko. "Sit."

Inhaling, Athena lifts her head and opens her eyes. Like a magnet, her irises dart in my direction.

Breathe. Just breathe.

Athena's lips spread into a wide grin accompanied by a few bashful blinks of soft eyes and a faint rosy blush to her cheeks.

I also blush.

I've never felt such warmth.

She's just figured out who I am.

She takes a step towards the only open seat on the left—the one right across from me and right next to Levi sitting at the head of the table. With a stern brow, she makes eye contact with each of the others. She slowly lowers her arse in the chair, also pursing her lips to each of them so they know just how angry she is.

Once I'm fully seated, the awkward silence is broken by Henry's moving hands.

"Let's eat!" cheers Shelley.

Laughter and cheers erupt as the clamor of dishes—forks against plates and toasts between glasses—resounds. But Athena refrains from joining in on the conversation as well as the meal. She doesn't eat. She doesn't speak. She doesn't move. I believe she must be in somewhat of a shock. A few questions land on her ears, but she just nods, unable to understand what is truly being asked of her. She probably wouldn't be able to articulate an answer anyway. I doubt she's ever envisioned meeting me, as a *human*, this way.

After sitting and fidgeting with her hands planted in her lap for a time, I decide to prop some creamy white dressed angel hair on her plate. She glances at my hand which holds the tongs, serving her pasta.

"You have big hands," she says softly.

"Mmm," I nod.

"You have many calluses. What type of work do you do?" She's questioning herself now—not entirely sure she trusts her instincts telling her I am who she thinks I am.

"I'm a sailor," I say boldly, "or I was." I don't know why she won't just ask me my name. Perhaps she is afraid of how she will behave in front of the gentleman she's brought if the truth were to hit her abruptly.

"A sailor you say?" She forces a grin. "I can see that."

"Can you now?"

"Mhm."

"So, tell me, miss, what else do you see?"

"It's embarrassing." She blushes. "I won't say."

"Please, as I mentioned earlier I've been gone for quite some time. Humor me, why don't you?"

"Well… um… for one, you have very hairy arms."

It's taking much strength to control my laugh as Levi chokes on his pasta.

"And what does a man's hair on his arms have anything to do with sailing?" I ask.

"Your hair is hardly noticeable except up close because it's been bleached by the sun to a near transparent blond." Her eyes wander from my forearm up to my bicep as I reach to clench more pasta and drop more noodles on her plate.

"I think that's enough for her." Levi shields Athena's plate of dangling noodles. A towering heap nearly touches her chin and I sigh, returning the tongs to the plate.

Athena and I make eye contact, which is quickly broken by Levi's head leaning forward across the table as he reaches for bread. The man winks, planting bread atop Athena's heap of pasta. "Hey babe, you okay?"

Babe? As in baby? Did he just call her a baby?

She blushes at the pet name. "I'm fine, thank you."

"You want some salad?" I chime in, grabbing a smaller plate and tossing some lettuce drizzled with dressing named after a Roman king, parmesan, and a few bread cubes. "You'll like this. I've tried some while my host was making it earlier," I boast, cocking my head to Shelley who blows a kiss my way. "I had no idea lettuce could be mixed with sauce and cheese or crisp stale bread in such a way that is pleasing."

"I have had Caesar salad before. Thank you." Athena smiles.

"Would you like a little extra parmesan?" asks Levi, reaching for the block of aged cheese and the grater. "She likes extra parmesan." He nods before he begins to grate, covering her pasta.

"That's enough," she says, watching Levi put the block and grater down, which I pick up.

"Have a little more on your salad as well." As I grate, a smile plays at the corner of Athena's mouth.

"Enough!" interrupts Levi, catching the attention of the rest of the table, which becomes awkwardly silent once again as all eyes glare at loads of shredded cheese smothering Athena's salad like thick snow leaving no trace of the earth after a blizzard.

"That's enough, don't you think?" Levi has his hands up, his elbows on the table.

"Forgive me." I place the cheese and grater down looking Athena in the eyes. "When you've been at sea as long as I, you can't wait to have your fill of everything."

"I'm sure Athena does not want to overindulge. If she gets too full too fast, then she might get tired and I'll have to take her home early." He rubs her shoulder. "I certainly don't want to do that. Small, simple pleasures, one at a time. That's how I believe Athena likes things. Huh, babe?"

There he goes, calling her *babe* again.

She blushes shamefully.

It irritates me. "Overindulgence is not something you concern yourself with but rather fantasize about when you're at sea, especially when it comes to women," I confess. "Small, simple pleasures are fine, but grand gestures—big and strong—are the tools I use to win a woman's heart." I give Athena a wink. "Indulgence—that has always worked for me."

"And how many women's hearts have you indulged?" Athena glowers wild-eyed.

"Many," I admit. "But like I said, I've been away and I—"

"What do you do with them?" She cocks her head, squinting.

"With what?"

"The hearts of the women you've won."

"He breaks them!" shouts Orphelius taking a gulp of more beer.

That drunk bastard!

"Is that true? Do you break their hearts once you've won them?" Athena's question spurs a pang in my chest.

"Does it matter?" interrupts Levi. "He's a sailor and we all know the stereotype. They have no home other than what lies across the horizon. But when it comes to women, they'll go wherever their compass points them."

Henry waves his hands around.

Shelley interprets. "Henry says you talk as though you have some experience as a seaman yourself, Levi."

Levi pushes on the bridge of his glasses to lift them up his nose. "I sail."

"For what purpose? Work? Pleasure?" I ask.

"I move cargo."

"Alone or—"

Levi leans back in his chair. "I have a superior."

"So, how many hearts have you and your superior broken?" I wonder. I know how lonely it can be at sea.

Levi looks to Athena. Her shoulders are raised, her arms are crossed, and she's hugging her own elbows. She is anxiously awaiting an answer.

Levi taps his fingers across the table's top. "None."

"Liar," I growl.

Levi clears his throat. "Excuse me?"

My voice turns low. "You're a fucking demon."

"That's rude!" Athena barks, standing up.

I stand up, too, kicking my chair over.

She huffs. "You can't call my date a demon." She seeks help from the others, searching their stunned faces. "He can't call my date a demon. Tell your *Captain* he can't call my date a demon."

"Captain?" Levi stands up, rubbing Athena's shoulder

again and I swear to the gods, I want to break his arm. "Hey, it's okay," he assures her. "We should leave."

"What?" She blinks. "No, I can't. I have to make the flyers."

"You don't have to do anything," says Levi.

Athena rubs her forehead, wincing. "I-I'm sorry Levi, but I have to stay and I'm so sorry if you feel insulted."

"I'm not insulted." The demon has his fingers wrapped around her upper arm pulling her toward him as he continues. "In fact, I don't even know these people, so I don't really care what they think or say about me."

"You *should* care," Orphelius tips his near empty mug in Levi's direction.

Levi wraps his hand around the back of Athena's neck, pulling her even closer. "And why is that?"

"Because you don't just have your hand wrapped around our Captain's prize but the very thing he believes *is* his horizon. And like you said, a seaman never ceases to chase what lies beyond, so I'm warning you. Our Captain's compass leads straight to that girl you've got your claws on."

Levi points between Athena and me. "So, you two know each other? Because I was under the impression you didn't know this guy."

"I don't." Athena talks calmly, grabbing Levi's hand, pulling it from her neck to hold it. "I've never laid eyes on this...," she waves her other hand up and down in front of me, "before tonight."

"So, you've never spoken with him?" asks Levi.

Athena gulps. "Well... y-yes I have."

Levi's face turns sour. "What's going on? Why do I feel like I'm being played? Am I in some staged mind game?"

Athena shakes her head. "No, nothing like that."

Levi steps up to Athena. I can sense the agitation in his demeanor. "Then what? You need to tell me or I'm leaving."

"We're a..." All heads lean in closer. *Is Athena about to spill the beans?* "The seamen are all from…" She fumbles with her skirt. "The captain, he's a… uh…"

A bell rings repeatedly, which is odd as the sound seems to be coming from Levi's trousers. He pulls out a device, which I have learned everyone seems to carry on land for quick communication, called a *cell*, and he speaks into it.

"Yeah… sure…" He huffs. "I'm on my way."

Levi stuffs his phone back into his pocket and grabs Athena by the chin. "I'm sorry, I have to go. Work." He tugs her hand, pulling. "Come on, I'll take you home."

She halts dead in her tracks. "I can't go. I have to stay and finish the flyers."

"For the sheriff? I wouldn't worry about him. He's more of a pussycat than a lion. I'm sure you can roll one over on him."

"I have to finish, Levi. Not just for him. But for the girls, the girls that are missing. I should have had these flyers done and put up yesterday."

Levi looks around the table. "I'm not sure I want to leave you with…" He cocks his head at the rest of us around the table, "them."

"They're my friends. I'll be fine."

He wraps his hand around the back of her neck again (I really need to just break his arm). Pulling her in, he speaks softly, "Are you sure about that? They don't act like they're your friends. They all seem to talk to you like you're an outsider."

"Regardless." She pulls his elbow, walking him to the front door and opening it. "I still need their help if I'm going to finish tonight."

"Fine." His eyes gloss over her lasciviously and I'm thankful the bootlicker has to leave. I just wish he'd hurry the fuck up and go, but instead, he pauses to ask, "Athena, you know I like you, right? Despite the age difference."

She smiles.

I'm tempted to walk over there and kick him in the arse! Right out the door!

He kisses her and my heart crash lands onto the floor. My eyes feel like they've just caught on fire. The young man spins her so her back is to me and he's facing the rest of us. Wrapping both hands behind her head, he kisses Athena more passionately and I'm about to look away until Levi makes eye contact with me.

He's kissing her while he's looking at me, and although I should be upset, a breeze passes through the beach house, putting me at ease.

Being a seaman isn't always about sailing. Being a commander of the high seas is most certainly not.

To divide and conquer—*that* is what was always expected of me by my superiors—to *divide and conquer* is the only reason a man would ever want to be Captain.

I smile at the demon.

This is going to be fun!

What a wonderful game this demon and I are going to play.

No, tis not a game.

This is going to be a war.

A war I intend to win.

My gods! It feels so *good* to be a man again.

10

ATHENA

Shock. I believe I'm in a state of shock.

The hard-press of Levi's lips on mine electrifies my body while his hands at the back of my head are coaxing me into the storm he is arousing in my core.

But there is a pull, tugging me from behind, in an opposite direction to keep away from the storm, away from the lightning.

The embarrassment of being kissed so hard in front of my hosts forces me to pull away from Levi. With a sucking sound, our lips come apart and I'm even more embarrassed when Levi cups my face and attempts to kiss me again.

I turn my head away, pretending I need to catch my breath.

"Walk me to my car?" asks Levi flashing those puppy dog eyes at me again.

Of course, I can't resist. "Yeah sure," I say, as he takes my hand and pulls.

Once we are clear of the house, Levi's tone turns gravelly. "Athena, I'm not so sure I want to leave you here. I think I'd rather take you home."

"The flyers," I say.

"Screw the flyers," he says, pulling on my arm until we are flush against one another and his hand is behind my head. "I don't want to leave you in the company of that... *guy*."

"Which guy?" I ask nonchalantly although I know exactly which guy Levi is talking about. I just want Levi to believe I'm not giving Willis any thought.

"The *big* guy. I still don't understand what's going on between the two of you but it's obvious he likes you and I don't like that."

In truth, I'm excited to know that Levi is feeling a little possessive over me, and I wonder if it's because he genuinely likes me, which is why he's behaving so protectively.

"You don't have to worry about the Captain." I offer a sweet show of gleaming teeth.

"The *Captain*," Levi scoffs. "Just hearing you say that makes me…" His jaw tenses as he shows me his gritting front teeth.

"Why are you so worried?" I ask, now feeling unsure of Levi's intentions. The tone in his voice and the anger deepening in his face makes me think Levi might be the *too* overly protective type, which I'm not so sure I like.

He sees the caution in me and the tense grip he has on the back of my head loosens. "I just… after what you told me earlier about you never having been with anyone before, I guess I just don't want to see you… you know?"

"Know what?" I want to hear him say what I think he's about to say.

He pulls my head into his chest and whispers in my ear. "You're perfect and pure and I don't want to see you ruined in any way. You're beautiful. I want to see what you look like underneath your clothes. Promise me you'll stay pure until you've given me a chance to..." He squeezes.

The heat radiating between Levi and myself is causing me to melt. I blink up at him.

"Promise me," he repeats.

"I promise," I say sincerely.

Levi lifts my chin with a finger to plant a kiss on my lips. I find myself swaying, my hips twirling back and forth with my hands behind my back pressed in silent prayer as he lets go.

Yes, I'm praying as I watch Levi get into his car and drive away. The way he makes me feel—*adored*—it must be genuine, although I wonder what type of work he does. I thought he was a student, but he's never mentioned coursework. Just the word, "work."

Laughter explodes from behind me causing the shack to shake. All those little sparks which Levi has left me with are quickly extinguished when I realize the purpose for which I am here. As Levi's tail lights get smaller and disappear into the dark night, I recognize how isolated Shelley's blue shack is along this patch of seacoast.

I wonder if the girls who the sheriff suspects have been abducted are okay. I also wonder where in the world they could possibly be and who in all the world could have taken them. *Why* would someone take them?

A breeze passes over my body, the chill wraps its arm around my shoulders. More laughter erupts from in the shack and I turn to hurriedly make my way back in but I stop when I see a large brooding shadow ahead.

Captain Willis has his arms crossed. He stands with his legs far apart. The light of the shack's interior from behind him makes his details difficult to make out but I know it's him. He so large.

For the life of me, I can't figure out why I feel like I'm about to get in trouble. Of course, it shouldn't matter to

Willis about what happened between Levi and myself but I feel shameful knowing Willis was watching us *kiss*.

I take a few steps towards the beach house and I see Willis's head rotate above his bulky shoulders as he watches me get closer to him. I look at his legs again.

Legs!

Covered with flesh!

And muscle. Thick muscle.

He shouldn't intimidate me but he does. This form he's in —as a man—is more intimidating than when he was in the shape of ice or a wall of water. For someone who has not walked in centuries, his has an incredibly sure and strong stance.

Oddly, I feel guilty. I'm trying to figure out how and why the captain came to acquire legs. *And why is here suddenly?*

I pause, stopping to stand but two feet away from him, although I don't look at him. We both say nothing but I can hear him breathing. In and out the air moves through his body and I'm wondering how he feels about it. *Breathing*. I would think he would be rejoicing—skipping, running, hanging out in the house with the other seamen laughing.

Instead of being out here with me.

I take a chance to glance in his direction but quickly look back down at my toes. From what I saw in the dark—one downwardly angled brow with the other raised, Willis looks angry. The sand beneath his bare feet stirs and his breathing picks up.

"I'm disappointed," he says.

I rub my arms. "Oh? About what?"

Is he not happy that he's human now? Or is he upset that I rejected his jewels?

I finally look Captain Willis in the eyes. Beautiful eyes I've known forever are even more beautiful now that they are in their sockets, sparkling like diamonds in a dark cavern.

"That kiss the demon gave you—it was weak." He smirks.

"The demon?" I cross my arms.

"Levi," he says lowly. "He doesn't know how to kiss a woman properly."

"Oh, and I supposed you do," I scoff. "I'm sure you know a lot about kissing women. Like you were saying, I'm sure you've kissed a lot of women, whoring women, back in your days before..." I spy his legs again.

"Aye," he nods. "I do. I did."

I swallow. Willis is nothing like I thought he would be. He's much more... I don't know... rough? Tough? Egocentric and... *manlier* than I thought he would be. I thought he would be sweet, humbled by the curse that's contained him for centuries.

Clearly not.

I march back towards the shack entrance. "Well, I'm not that kind of girl."

"I know, and I'd like to keep it that way," he says, bending forward as I cross his path. I'm not exactly sure what he's doing when he picks me up, throwing me over his shoulder.

"Hey!" I shout, smacking his back. *What the hell does he think he's doing?*

"Don't fight, Athena. The goddess of wisdom was not made to fight but she was made to be won. You need a real kiss. A strong kiss, but I need to wash that demon filth from you first."

Wash that demon filth? What in the world?

Straining my neck to lift my head, I see we are headed past the beach house and towards the shore. Willis's strides are long but smooth. He seems calm and at ease, which is the opposite of what I'm feeling. My pulse is racing.

Within seconds we are at the shoreline and my heart has fallen into my throat. I yelp, clawing and then twisting at Willis's shirt.

I think he is about to throw me in the water!

"Willis," I cry out as his strides slow against the waves pummeling against his shins and then his knees and his thighs.

He pulls at me—my legs—which are trying to remain wrapped tight, clenched around him as my hands are now pulling at the waistline of his jeans above his ass.

"Willis, damn you. I don't want to get wet. Plea—"

Too late.

With both of his hands lifting me at my hips, I am tossed to find myself in the air and then head underwater.

Kicking my feet and waving my arms, I try to get my bearings so that I may swim to the surface. But instead, I am grabbed at the wrist and pulled. Quickly, my head emerges and before I can blink an eye, a finger—a *thumb*—is at my mouth.

I poke out my tongue trying to spit out the thumb that is now invading me. I twist my hands around Willis's massive forearm, trying to get him to stop. More fingers make their way into my mouth and I feel like he's scrubbing away at the interior.

Trying to fight him, I squeal, "Sto—," but only find myself completely submerged, pushed underwater once again.

Willis repeats this process, pulling me to him to wash out my mouth and scrub over my lips and then inside my oral cavity before he pushes me under again and again. And just when I think I can't take anymore because I can't breathe, Willis's tongue finds my own and we are kissing.

I'm not surprised to find the Captain has lied. There's nothing "proper" about his kiss at all. His tongue reaches so far back into my throat that I have to push on him. And he's groping me. His hands squeeze at my hips, my sides, and he claws at my ass.

He grabs my breast and now, I can't breathe! My lungs are about to collapse under his touch.

Fighting for a gasp of air, I inhale deeply when he finally withdraws his tongue only to lick up my neck.

The sensation forces my back to arch up and into him. He groans as his tongue slithers back to my lips—this time his tongue tip slips repeatedly in and out of my mouth with a sweet little suckle and I melt. His arms snake around my waist to keep me supported.

He squeezes. His thick arms make me feel so thin and fragile. He could break me if he wished. His kiss comes harder again. His arousal is also hard at my thigh and I push on him more firmly, pulling my mouth away.

That...

That was a kiss.

"Captain," I exhale, looking into his eyes and remembering his curse as he holds me loosely. "If you wish to stay a man, you must lay with a woman."

He puts his nose to mine before he chomps on my bottom lip and tugs. "Two days," he growls and drops me.

Down I go, waving my arms around and desperately trying to get my feet planted on the ocean's bottom once again. When I finally pop up to smear seawater away, I see the Captain's back is already to me.

Isn't this just like him! He's kissed me and has immediately put his back to me.

"Willis, what do you mean 'two days?' Where are you going? Why are you leaving me again? Why will you never talk to me?"

"Because I'm at war," he shouts back, "A captain never gives away his battle plans and I only have two days. Two days to make you fall in love with me and not the *me* you've been obsessing about your whole life, but the *me* that is in front of you now. The *me* that needs to win this war and put down your demons."

Shelley is sweet enough to let me shower and lend me some clothes. By the time we are nearly finished with the flyers, I realize how tired I am after enduring all the events of the evening. I didn't kiss one but *two* men and although each kiss felt right, I must say the second one left me in a doozy.

I'm still trying to understand exactly what Willis meant with his *war* speech and why he keeps referring to Levi as a demon.

I've also made several attempts to find out by asking Willis exactly how he was able to transform back into a man, but he is reluctant to give any details. He simply ignores me as the other seamen do whenever I ask for insight. I don't understand because there's no way I'm going to fall in love with someone who is going to continue to ignore me, keep me out of the loop just as he did before.

As the last round of flyers is drafted, I catch myself yawning and ask Shelley if she wouldn't mind taking me home. But she yawns too, which triggers a round of yawns to circle between fatigued women and drunken seamen.

Kumiko suggests that I stay for the night, which I reluctantly agree to do. I tell myself I'm only staying because heaven forbid anyone should get into an accident due to sleepiness on my account.

Naturally, I take it upon myself to finish the last of the flyers, which means I'm the last to emerge from the restroom, with my glasses, and ready to go to bed. Of course, there are no beds left, only a patch-worked couch which is occupied by a burly, blond seaman who is half naked and grinning, wearing only a pair of briefs that must belong to one of the other men because it is clearly too small for him. The crown of his bulge is ready to rip through. He holds a blanket with one arm held up in the air like a welcome sign inviting me to take the only open spot left available—on the couch, in his arms.

"Come now, Athena," he says, as I shuffle with my feet.

"Maybe you should sleep on the floor," I suggest.

"Ha," he laughs, peeping over the edge to look at the wood floors before he looks me over. "This is my first night back among the civilized. I want cushions. I *deserve* cushions," he groans. "Bring it here."

Bring it? As in bring *myself?*

"You're not at all what I thought you were going to be."

"No." He lets go of the blanket and strokes his hair back. "And I tried to warn you. I turned you away many times. But here I am. Because of your persistence."

"Are you saying *I'm* the reason you're here?"

"Aye," he acknowledges.

I'm unsure if I should be happy or remorseful he went through the trouble. "You made a deal with the witch, didn't you?"

"Aye, but we're not discussing that tonight." He reaches

his hand out, curling his fingers, signaling me towards him. "Come. Rest with me. I have not slept for centuries. I had no idea I'd missed the feeling of my body eager to rest. All these sensations I'd forgotten are overwhelming. Come, lay with me. Tell me a story. Whisper to me. Let me hear you with my own ears."

I'm the reason he's here. I'm the reason he's here. I'm the reason.

I repeat the words in my mind like a chant, remembering this is what I thought I wanted but I'm dying to know.

What did it cost?

I decide to lie down. My eyelids are so heavy and although the Captain did scrub my mouth out with his fingers *and* his tongue, I get the feeling he's not going to do it again. At least, not tonight.

When I approach, I turn my back to him before I place my glasses on the side table and plant my butt down, lifting my legs and leaning my shoulders downward to nestle my back into him. His thick arm folds over me before he pulls me tight and flush against his heat.

The house quickly falls silent and all I hear is the air—Willis's air—blowing over my ears along with the ocean spreading its reach over the shore outside.

But my ever-curious mind cannot rest. "What is it like to be made of water?"

"*You* are mostly made of water," Willis replies. "What does it feel like to you?"

"Please," I chortle. "You know, it's not the same."

"No," he says, sneakily moving his hand over my breast to cup it, which makes me pant. "Mmm," he massages. "It's most definitely not." He nuzzles his face into the back of my neck. "A story, Athena," he begs. But before I can even open my mouth, he lets out a snore.

11

ATHENA

Two days. That's what he said. He said he has two days, but I'm curious as to exactly when those two days begin and end.

Are we talking forty-eight hours? Or is this a Cinderella thing where he'll be forced to return to the sea at midnight tonight?

I can't believe how large he is. As a block of ice, so smooth, he seemed less elongated than he looks now with all those mounds of flesh rippling when he moves. I can't stop looking at him.

And it's annoying because other people can't stop looking at him as well. *Women* won't stop ogling.

The gang decided that we would go into town. The seamen love riding in cars. walking on sidewalks, and pushing buttons of crosswalk signs.

I'm not surprised to see all the common things, which I have little appreciation for, Willis finds intriguing. I find it very funny that the thing Willis loves the most is ice cream. In fact, he ends up eating three double scoop cones of six different flavors. When his face becomes a mess of sticky scruff, I finally have to cut him off. I also end up paying for it all, although I don't really mind as I know the Captain is much wealthier than me. With all that treasure he has on his secret island, I'm sure the man is worth millions.

For an hour, we stroll through Main Street. After we've had our fill of snacks, the other couples decide to go on their own way, although I do believe Willis is the reason I find myself alone with him, strolling through the streets and sightseeing.

"Do all of the people of this time hold hands like that," he asks, pointing to several couples, tourists mostly, holding hands. A young couple, an elderly couple, and even a young mother and father with a baby strapped into a carrier on the father's back are holding hands.

"Yes, I guess it's common."

"That's very interesting," says Willis, rubbing his jaw. "In my time, such affection between a man and a woman, such *closeness*, would've been frowned upon. Unless of course…" He bites his lip.

"Unless what?" I'm very curious.

"Unless they were in a brothel."

I can feel his gaze on me. He's waiting for a reaction.

I try to remain calm. I should give him the benefit of the doubt. He is after all from another time and I am well aware of the activities of the men of his day. I am an expert, after all, on such behavior of his times.

"Did you visit many of them?" I ask. "Brothels?"

From the corner of my eye, I see him lick his lip before he stands up straight, sticking his chest out. "I did. Does that bother you?"

I can't for the life of me figure out why we are having such a conversation. I'd always thought that if I'd had a chance to meet Willis in person I'd be asking him about all the things he could do with his powers of water motion. I'd ask him about the creatures, especially the magical ones, the ones I cannot see, which he's kept in his domain. I'd ask him about history and all the things he's witnessed—great militaries battling against one another during the great wars and what followed after the birth of my country.

"Why are we talking about brothels?" I scowl.

"Because I have two days," he says and stops. "Look at that." He points with excitement.

We have come to the end of Main Street that widens into a curved street with a turn off that heads straight towards a small bay. "The marina?"

"Can we go there?" He puts his hand against his forehead to shadow his eyes from the sun overhead so that he may see better.

This is very odd. Willis has not been away from the sea but for a few hours and it seems he is ecstatic to return. "Why would you want to go to the marina?" I ask. "There are only boats there."

"Yes," he says excitedly. "I have not been on a ship for far too long. Come, my goddess, let me see what the fine tech… techo…techno... what was that word Shelley used?"

"Technology?"

"Yes," he grabs my hand and pulls. "Let's see what advancements your *techno-no* has made for me."

The man is giddy as we stroll along the docks. He behaves like a young boy in a toy store. The Captain cannot keep his hands off each boat he chooses to inspect. Of course, he aims to stroke the bellies of the shiniest, most expensive looking boats and I guess I can't blame him for wanting to smooth his hands across each well-crafted vessel. I'd forgotten he has not touched a ship with human fingers in over two hundred years.

We stumble into an old man who appears to be shining

up the front end of his fancy boat. "Would you like some help with that, sir?" asks Willis.

The old man and Willis start talking—*sailor* talk—I can't understand a thing or if the conversation is going well with all the squinting and shinnying up of mechanisms going on between them. The old man seems delighted and genuinely impressed with Willis. I'm able to just sit and relax, watching the seagulls dive bomb for food for some time under a small shaded canopy to keep my sunburn from getting worse. But with a friendly handshake, it appears the men have come to some sort of agreement.

Of all the things Willis could ask for, although I'm not completely surprised, he comes over to tell me that he needs money. *A thousand dollars exactly!* Just to take the old man's boat out for a few hours.

It's difficult to agree when I realize I don't even have that much cash. I'm a *librarian* paid by the town, a *small* town, which can't really afford a library, and which also means I can hardly afford dinner at a fancy restaurant, let alone would I pay for a few hours on what looks like an overpriced private yacht with all of its fancy gadgets, except I'm assured it's a sailboat.

Willis sees the contemplation in my face. "Is that a lot?" he asks. "The old man says he's given me a bargain. He says he normally charges twice that. Is he trying to swindle me?"

"No, it's okay." I shudder inside. "But will you ask him if he takes a credit card. I can only pay if he'll take a credit card."

"The man says he takes all forms of payment, but we must pay in advance."

Willis is smiling as we make our payment transaction via the old man's cellphone. Willis is in awe. Never would I have thought in all my studies that meeting a merman would amount to paying for a field trip at sea in luxury.

Once we have paid, the old man shows Willis how to start and stop the engine and then, within a few minutes, Willis and I are at sea.

The man is beaming. The second we make it far enough from shore, the wind picks up, the sails come down, and Willis is hollering. The wind blows through his hair and I swear he looks like something out of a scene in the movie, *Titanic*, especially the scene where Jack and Rose are at the bow. It's the scene where the couple truly fall for one another romantically right before they decide to get freaky in the backseat of a 1912 Renault Town Car. Of course, I know these details because I'm obsessed with all movies related to the ocean, but right now, I'm regretting watching that movie over a million times.

It's clear that although Willis has been tied to the sea and could still very well be for eternity, the man loves the ocean. I consider perhaps that Willis had not been cursed worse than the other seamen, but instead gifted his greatest love.

I could never be his Rose.

"What are you thinking about over there?" questions Willis, leaving the helm as the boat slows.

"Nuh... nothing," I hum lowly as he removes his shirt, tossing it aside.

His muscles are rippling again. They gleam as they flex under the midday sun while he moves swiftly this way and that to lower the sails with yanks on ropes and pulleys to slow us down.

He drops the anchor.

"Why are we stopped?" I ask standing up from my seat.

"There are sharks up ahead." He raises a brow.

My knees get weak and I have a sudden urge to cling onto something. I instinctively grab onto him. "Sharks?"

"Aye, see there." He points to a place in the water where I can definitely make out fins. *Two*. No. *Three!* Fins.

"What are they doing?" I ask, clawing into the muscleman beside me.

He removes my hands, getting behind me, and pushing me further towards the bow.

My feet, reluctant and fighting with shaky resistance, don't want to move any closer to the edge than they have to.

"Take a look," he says. "I believe they are feeding. They must've caught something." Willis nudges me more forward in front of him, placing each of his hands at my hips.

"Captain?" I sway, wrapping my fingers tight around his wrists. The last time Willis held me like this with his fingers digging into my hip bones was last night right before he tossed me into the ocean to scrub my face of what he thought was demon's spit.

Willis nuzzles his nose through my hair until his lips find my ear. "We should go for a swim."

What? Is he crazy!

I jerk back. My bottom, dressed in loose white linen shorts I had to borrow from Shelley this morning, bangs against Willis's groin.

"I'm not swimming with a bunch of hungry sharks out there." I try to scoot forward out of embarrassment, but his hands keep my butt planted against him.

"There's a hungrier shark on board," he growls.

I'm not sure how to respond. *Should I laugh? Cry? Gag?* The Captain is not so smooth as I thought he was because that was the cheesiest pickup line I think I'd ever heard in my life.

I cock my head. "If you're trying to flirt with me, saying you're a hungry shark is hardly—"

"I wasn't talking about me," he interjects, pushing on my hips with his hands to create some distance between us. And now, I can't deny that I wish I played along. As I watch him take a seat, propping his arm over the side of the boat and pulling a knee up—so confident but so relaxed—he finishes, "I was talking about *you*."

"Me?" I point to myself.

He smiles widely with a squint of one eye. "Aye, *you*. You're worse than a shark. You scare me a little—always coming around every summer since you were little. Trying to tempt me, lure me into showing myself to you. A little monster you were—so stubborn, so *foreboding*." His eyes gravitate to my mouth. "And those teeth! Like razors, they scare me. Show me one of those shark teeth."

I cover my mouth, mumbling. "I don't have shark teeth!"

He laughs, leaning forward to grip my fingers. "Come here." He pulls, dropping his knee so that my butt lands on his lap. Swiping his finger over my cheek, Willis pulls a tendril of my hair away from my face before he takes off my glasses, putting them atop a cooler I hadn't noticed earlier beside him.

He pulls at my chin so that I am facing him and he runs his thumb across my cheek. "I know this face," he says. He strokes his index finger down my chin, my neck, and my chest. "After all that gibberish I've heard from you over the years, I also know too well this soul and all that is desired by this heart." He taps at the space between my breasts.

Pulling his hands away, Willis reaches behind me, cupping my bottom cheeks and blinks as he looks up at me. "I want to know this body as well, Athena, but you don't know me at all. Why have you pledged your body to me when you have no idea who I really am, who I *was*? I've been around for a long time. I'm really just an old man whereas you..." He licks his lips as his eyes travel downward. "You still have your youth."

Youth? Jesus, I'm thirty. In fact, physically, the Captain is so ripped and sexy, he looks younger than me. I'm confident he is humanly younger than me.

My finger circles his shoulder.

"Don't do that," he says seeking my hand, but I slap his away and continue.

"Don't do what?" I respond trailing my fingers up a shoulder to his neck and through his hair where I let my fingertips graze.

"I haven't been touched in a long time, Athena." He leans his face into my neck, speaking, "If you continue to touch me like this, without being absolutely sure this is what you want, I might have to feed you to the sharks."

"This is what I want, Willis."

He grabs my hips again. "You don't know that. You don't know me," he says as he begins to rock his hips upward, his groin grinding against my swelling folds. "You want the magic and the mystery. You want the *merman*. Not me."

I cup his face, forcing him to look me in the eyes. "The merman, *this* man—you are both the same."

He shakes his head. "I wish that were true. For your sake, I wish that were true. But I'm not. You need to learn this. I'll show you," he says and comes to standing, lifting me and then throwing me overboard.

For heaven's sake!

Into the air, I go screaming and kicking my feet until I am lost deep underwater. Swiftly, I push with all my energy to rise to the surface searching for Willis up above.

He wanders to the back of the boat, tearing off his pants to be fully naked, and swinging a step ladder over the side.

I swim to the ladder, but I am quickly cut off. My path is interrupted by Willis diving in with his arms outstretched straight over his head and toes pointed. A perfect 10.0.

He swims to me with his sights set behind me. "Look out," he says calmly, "there's a shark behind you."

What?

My body is overtaken with fear as I turn to see a shark fin is truly headed in my direction. I scream!

My waist is looped and pulled by Willis's arm, but the save is not enough to keep me from screaming again! All of my natural instincts say to run, swim away, get to the ladder before I'm eaten up. But Willis keeps me trapped in his arms as he tries to calm me down.

"They're not going to hurt you."

"The hell they are!" I push on him.

"I swear to you, they are not. The witch— she has reign over them."

A moment ago, I was fighting against Willis to get to safety, but now I find myself clinging to him as the other sharks also head our way. "And how do you know she won't stop them from chewing us up to tiny bits? How do you know she doesn't want us *dead*?"

Willis pulls me in front of him to cradle my face. "The deal I made. The witch needs me alive. She needs us both to break the curse, so she will have my powers. We have nothing to fear of these beasts which she controls. But Athena…" His eyes turn a deeper gray.

"But?" We are afloat, and I get the feeling we are about to sink.

"Magic has a cost," he groans. "To be with you for these two days and become fully human and without powers, I had to pay."

Pay? He's done something. He's made a deal. A deal I fear even more than the sharks circling around us. "What did you do? What price are you going to pay?"

Willis's eyes bore into me. "Athena, whether you choose to lay with me or not, whether I become a man or must return to the ocean when my two days are over, I will not be able to see. I traded my eyes."

I slam the water with both arms, splashing. "Why would you do that?"

"You were in danger."

"Danger?" My eyes zig-zag back and forth until they veer straight into the small space between us. "Levi? You did this because of *Levi*? Because you think he's a *demon*?"

Willis nods.

I can't believe this. "The witch has tricked you. Levi's no demon. He's a goody-two-shoes. A nerd. He'd never hurt a fly. I can't believe you let that witch trick you into giving up your eyesight. Goddamn you, Willis!"

I swim away to the ladder. The sharks clear out of my path.

This is craziness. Yes, I'm the number one believer in all this hocus pocus, but even this *is too crazy for me.*

Both sets of my fingers curl over the bottom step made of aluminum. Pulling my legs in to help myself climb upward, my ankles are snatched. I turn around, still hanging on, to see Willis has them.

His face is halfway under water. Only his eyes—fixed, narrow, beaming, hungry—I see. He looks hungrier than the sharks swimming by. He parts my ankles, pushing them apart and pulls, using them as leverage to glide in between my legs. When he is flush against me, front against front, he wraps my legs around him and grabs my hips.

"You're not getting away from me. I went through a lot of trouble to get here," he growls.

"Yeah, and I spent a lot of *money* to get here."

"Hmm, so it *was* a lot." His eyes glaze over my lips. "But not worth what you paid, is it?"

"A thousand dollars is not worth this arguing."

He swipes his wet thumb down my cheek. "We're not arguing."

I grit my teeth. "Then, what do you call this?"

"This..." he kisses me gently, "is a lovers' quarrel."

I'm melting. I'm instantly about to become one with the sea.

"Lover's quarrel?" I mutter through his wet hot lips. "There's no difference. It's still an argument," I say softly as Willis leans into me, tucking his nose into my neck.

"Aye." Willis curls his tongue under the sensitive flesh behind my ear as he grinds his bare erection along the split between my legs. "But this argument will end as all lovers' quarrels do—with me, a man, deep in his woman, which is you."

Me. His woman?

The crash of Willis's lips on mine—hard, sucking, enveloping—makes my toes curl. My knees come up, caging his ribs against me. My dripping, drenched shirt comes over my head and my bra is painfully snatched off. Clearly, he's not used to removing such an undergarment.

I yelp, so he kisses me harder, moving to my cheek, my jaw, my neck, and down to my chest. His head disappears beneath the surface. My nipple is lapped before it's bitten and sucked.

"Gentle," I cry out. Perhaps, I should reveal that I've never done this before.

Willis pops up, kneading my breast. "I've been waiting for this for much longer than you can imagine." He pinches my nipple, which makes my hips buck, and he grabs the globe of one of my bottom cheeks to claw into my flesh. "This is as gentle as I can get."

He kisses me again—hard. I'm whimpering into his mouth, desperate to hold onto the ladder, to not let go. It's my only path to safety that will keep me from getting in too deep.

Willis's hand scrolls flat down my front until his fingers find my slit, which feels swollen. He strokes up and down, barely in the crease, teasing, encroaching on my swollen nub but not quite touching the hardened little nub. He pauses to gather my knees to pull down my shorts and underwear.

"Willis," I whisper feeling the motion of a shark swimming by.

I open my eyes to look beyond Willis across the deep blue sea, into the horizon, as he spreads my legs around him again and invades me with his fingers. He pushes through my folds and into my core.

"Oh," I cry out, never having felt this before. There's so much intense pleasure filling my entire body as he threads his fingers in and out of me. It's a feeling I never would've suspected could come from the digits of a man's hand furrowing deep within.

But he withdraws, escaping me, and for a moment I'm in despair, feeling as if I've been marooned. But then he grabs my bottom and lifts my ass so my hips are above the water. My body aligns flat with the surface and my crease comes centered over his face.

"Mmm," he laps, digging his tongue inside me where his fingers once were.

I shudder, hanging on to the ladder while trying to keep my body upright as Willis licks right up my sea-watered slit to grind his tongue against my clit.

The sky above has never seemed so wide. Everything feels so big and wide. I feel like I could just float right up into the clouds, and...

Heavens, *I do.*

The moment I come, I feel high. The earth disappears as my body lets go, drifting upward.

I'm soaring!

The tongue that ties me down, however, reels me back in with an overwhelming, grounding sensitivity. I become so sensitive I can no longer let the Captain stay at the helm.

I clamp my legs together, drawing them in, and he smiles, proud of himself.

12

WILLIS

Beautiful. From the way the tendrils of her wet hair frames her face to the way her eyes sparkle, I have never seen this woman looking more beautiful than she does now. I especially love the look of humility she's wearing. She's embarrassed. I don't believe Athena has ever experienced such pleasure before and...

I hope she wants more.

I swim closer. "Did you like that?"

She bats her eyes. "I... I did."

I cup her breast rubbing my thumb over her nipple. "I liked it too. I want to eat more of you." I nibble on her chin.

The corners of her mouth quirk up as she continues to cling to the ladder with her hands above her. I reach up to stroke my hands down her arms, then down her sides.

She lets out a small moan, closing her eyes.

I wrap my arm around her back and lift her slightly so her breasts pop up above the surface where I take her teat in my mouth.

"Oh, jeez," she cries, her face clenching.

I pause from sucking on her hardened nipple. "What's the

matter?" I ask, although I know exactly what the matter is. I just want to hear it from her mouth.

Her eyes pop open. "I had no idea this was going to feel so good."

"It feels better coming from me, doesn't it?" I dip my head to swirl my tongue around her pale pink areola before I nip hard with my front teeth and tug a little.

"Mmm, yes," she gasps.

I capture her gaze, looking her straight in the face. "This is why you waited for me. Because deep down you knew better than both of us…" Trailing my fingers down her front, I continue, "You knew I was the only one who would ever be able to navigate you properly."

Athena's mouth gapes open as her eyes close when my finger finds her slit. Her chest is heaving and I can sense her grip is getting weak. Gliding the tip of my middle finger towards her entrance again, I barely graze her softened bud when her hips jerk. She's so sensitive, she can't hold on and her body slips to become fully submersed.

I laugh.

Grabbing onto the ladder myself with one hand and getting a hold of Athena with the other, I pull her up. She puffs, spraying water in my face before she takes a big gulp of air.

"I'm sorry," she cries even more embarrassed than she was before.

"My goddess should never be sorry," I smile, pulling her in by the back of her neck so I can kiss her lips. "I have every intention of making love to you *but*..." My head teeters. "Perhaps right now is not the right time."

"We need the compass."

Her eyes are so big, staring up at me. I feel as if I could dive right into them. I want to dive into her right now. The urge to plunge my swollen length into Athena is overwhelming. The feeling is more urgent than every second I've spent over centuries wishing I could walk on land again, but…

"That's right," I say. "We need the compass if I'm to remain in this form." I bite my lip.

"What's wrong?" She asks with a bob, going up and down, as small waves move between us.

"Is this really how you want me? Now, that you've seen me… what I look like… as a man… am I still what you want?"

Athena wraps her arms under mine, hooking them over my shoulder to pull her chest against me and plants a kiss in my neck. "You are what I want."

"I won't have powers. All the magic you are obsessed with, Athena, I will no longer possess and I will no longer be able to see. My face will appear disfigured. The sockets where my eyes should go will be empty."

"Your eyes are a permanent fixture in my mind. They made me who I am." She squeezes. "And it's not the magic that entices me but the sacrifices you made each time you were transformed. It's the sacrifices you made that makes the real magic happen."

I exhale, nudging her towards the ladder. "Come," I say. "Let's pull up the sails and head back to shore."

"Are you sure? We still have some time left. I did pay a lot," she says pulling herself up to hike up the ladder.

I revel, licking my lips as I watch the beautiful naked arse climbing upward right above me. I make sure I get a good look. This view is most certainly something I want to remember when my vision is gone.

"No, my love," I respond, following up the ladder. "Time was once my friend, but 'tis my enemy now." I swing my leg over the side of the boat to join Athena onboard, fronting her. "I will find a way to pay you back."

"You d-don't ha-have to," she stutters, ogling me—my

body. Though, I wonder if she's got a clear view. She's not wearing her spectacles, so I step closer.

Not surprisingly, I come to no longer exist. Once Athena's eyes have scanned over every ripple of my mass, she quickly forgets about her inspection. Except, of course, for the piece of me that dangles between my legs, the piece that has completely captivated her.

My hook.

The closer I step, the farther she moves away while keeping her sights transfixed on my stiff but curved sword. When I step back, she leans in, unconsciously trying to get a better look. I step towards her once more only to watch her bare feet stumble backwards again.

We do this dance until her back lands against the boat's side rails where she has nowhere left to go unless she wants to go overboard again, which I doubt. I'm sure she's more interested in getting eaten by me for a second time than by those sharks still swarming. What's interesting is how Athena has never feared me. Not after her fingers were burnt after touching me when I was a block of ice. Not when I first presented myself to her as a tidal wave. But me, in this form with my arousal fully thick and swollen, it makes her fingers tremble, her toes fidget, and her lips quiver.

Closing in on her, I take her hand, her *tremoring* hand, to wrap it around my hard shaft. She wraps her palm gently.

I take a breath.

Breathe. Just breathe.

The sensation of Athena's delicate fingers around my arousal sends a jolt of energy through my body. I fold my hand over hers. She can't clasp around the shaft fully, my hook is too thick, so I help her to fist up and down the full length of my erection.

I swallow. This feeling of intimacy—I've missed it. I've missed it worse than not being able to eat or drink. Worse than missing guzzling down a fine ale. I had been made of water, but I'd felt parched—unable to ingest just one drop of liquid and let alone taste anything.

I grab Athena by the face, pulling her in by the cheeks to kiss her as she continues to stroke me on her own. I lap up every bit of salt and spit that lingers over her lips and I swallow her essence again and again until I'm filled to the brim with ecstasy and I come, leaking and then exploding, splashing all over her front.

She says she doesn't like being sprayed, but she doesn't seem to mind this—my cum.

Athena's head tilts down to examine the creamy fluid splashed over her soft belly. She smears and rubs the fluid between her fingers as if she needs to study, *know*, every little bit about me.

Always the scholar this one. I love her. I clutch and kiss her again.

Grabbing a rag from a pile the boat's owner had left, I wipe Athena clean of the splash I've made. We are both giggling as I do this and the next thing I know we are tickling one another.

By the gods, it feels so good to be human! But it feels even better to be a man in love!

"Ah, fuck!" shouts an angry voice from behind. It's a familiar voice that is perhaps *too* angry and has the worst timing. It's a voice I know can only come from...

A demon.

I need to put Levi down. I know he's after my most perfect treasure, my Athena. I'll kill him if I have to, but the second I spin around, I get knocked in my chest.

I land hard and flat against the deck floor. I cannot breathe. I realize I wasn't knocked but hammered by something powerful, as if Poseidon had struck me by his own hand, knocking the wind right out of me.

Athena screams and I make an attempt to get up only to get knocked in the chest again, feeling a rib... or maybe two, crack within me.

What the hell is that he's beat me with?

Shielding my eyes from the glare of the midday sun, I see the demon, *Levi*, holding a bat similar to those held by children of my time playing cricket in the streets of my mother country, except Levi's bat is not flat or made of wood but fully rounded and made of metal.

"Watch him," shouts Levi to another man climbing aboard. Levi tosses the bat to the other, much larger man, who takes the bat and sizes me up.

I give him a wicked glare. *That's right, I'm much bigger than you and broken ribs or not, the second I take that weapon from you, I'll kill you.*

As if the man can read my mind—one killer to another—he hits the bat over my shoulder. I don't let the pain get to me. I reach for the weapon, ready to take it away, when Athena screams my name.

"Willis, don't!"

I turn to see my poor girl with a gun to her neck.

"Stay where you are," demands Levi. "Move and I'll kill her."

My anger burns with an unfathomable heat. Like a wild fire, my fury ignites. Athena, I fear was wrong and the witch, I hate to say, was right. This man *is* a demon. Only a demon could put Hell's fire in another's heart.

I'm desperate to climb out of this inferno, take that gun, shoot that demon, and then throw his evil arse overboard to become shark fodder. The bat and the gun—these things each seem hardly worthy of hesitation. I'm having difficulty containing myself from standing up and strangling both of these bootlicker's to death with my bare hands.

But I think of Henry and I remember what great pain and

destruction can result from something so small as a bullet. Looking at the gun pressed firmly against Athena's skull, I resign to roll over like a dog and stay flat on my back.

"That's more like it," says Levi, adjusting his glasses up his nose. He points his gun at me and yanks back on Athena's hair, speaking in her ear. "Did you fuck him?"

She's crying, trying to crisscross her arms over her naked body to conceal herself. "Wha-what?"

"Did you have *sex* with him?" Levi's tone is much louder and more intense.

"I absolutely fucked her," I lie.

"No, you didn't," Athena squeals, shaking her head. "Levi, I swear I didn't. We didn't have sex."

"Yes, we did." I raise my voice, trying to sound more convincing. "I fucked her long and hard and if you two had not shown up I would've fucked her in the arse as well."

"Willis!" she cries. "Why are you lying? Stop!"

Levi grunts. "Fuck, I have to check." The demon tips his chin up to his accomplice. "Help me. Hold her so I can open her legs."

I turn my head away as Levi does his inspection. Athena is screaming at the top of her lungs but I use the opportunity to lean up and search beyond the ship's edge for any sign of help. All I see is another boat, smaller and docked behind ours, which must belong to the two invaders. As if I had not learned my lesson from Athena's parents when she was younger, in the time I'd spent getting intimate with Athena, I'd put her in danger.

"She's still intact," says Levi. "Let's take her."

With those words, Athena has finally come to an understanding of what's happening. She's about to become one of the missing and she fights. But the fighting is useless. With one pour of a solution from a little bottle and into a handkerchief then placed over her face, Athena falls faint.

"You can't do this," I say. "She's innocent, a very sweet and innocent woman."

"Yes, I know," Levi says bending down to pick her up and throw her over his shoulder. "Which is why she is going to fetch a good price. Most buyers like 'em young, but a woman like this, this old, so soft and beautiful, but still preserved and untouched..." He taps her arse which makes my blood boil. "Athena is a true gem. Extremely rare. She'll go to a very high paying collector."

"You're not taking her," I warn, coming up on my knees and readying to attack.

"Oh, don't worry," Levi points the gun at me and fires.

A flaming burn shreds right through my neck. My hands are instantly at my own throat in reaction. Between my fingers I feel something and pull, tugging out whatever Levi shot me with. I prop it up, in front of my eyes, to look at it.

My vision is blurring and my speech is slurring. "Wha-what did you sh-shoot me with?" I ask because I know it's no bullet.

"A tranquilizing dart," Levi chortles and looks to his friend. "Bring him."

I try to resist, but I find I am useless as Levi's accomplice kicks on my shoulder, pushing me over to watch me land heavy and he laughs.

Levi laughs with him. "You're coming with us. Someone is desperate to meet you and the rest of your *kind*. I'm not just here for her. I'm also here for you, *Captain*."

For me? My kind? What does he mean? I know no one in this time. Why in the world would anyone want me?

As I watch Levi pick up Athena's glasses and become a blob as he strolls away with my girl over his shoulder, I feel a hand wrap around my wrist before I'm yanked and pulled across the deck.

My body is completely useless. *A tranquilizing dart* is what Levi said. He's drugged me.

As much as I try to fight against this feeling, a sensation I've never felt before, I fear I'm losing more than control over my appendages. I'm about to lose control of my mind, which goes blank.

I feel a kick to my foot.

"Hey, get up," says Levi.

I'd rather not. This throbbing in my head is pulsing with a most tortuous rhythm and my body feels so heavy that I don't care how cold this damp floor is...

What is that smell?

I gag with the scent of something so atrocious, it must be dead.

My eyes flip open to see the man who's abducted Athena. I'm in a dark room—underground, I suspect. The only light coming in beams brightly through a door atop a staircase.

Levi throws clothing at me. "Put these on," he says, still

holding a gun, although this one he has pointed at me looks different than the one from earlier.

I squint to get a good look. Levi's not standing that far away. My legs are still weak, but I bet I could still take him.

Levi taps his temple with the tip and points the gun back in my direction. "Don't do anything stupid," he warns. "This gun is not filled with darts. This gun will kill you. And believe me, I'd love to fucking kill you but I've been asked not to. Someone wants to meet you first. Now, get up and put those clothes on. I'm fucking sick and tired of looking at you."

I sit up with a chuckle. "I'd be sick too if I was you having to look at me. A little jealous, are we?"

My muscles constrict as a *BAM* sounds off. The sound is followed by a chorus of unharmonious wails.

"Don't piss me off, *freak!*" shouts Levi, who's just fired his gun, shooting the wall behind me.

As dust settles over my naked skin, I look around. I hadn't realized I was not the only one here. I make out a few feminine faces, most of them crying, most I don't know but...

My heart caves in when I see two women's faces that are familiar *and then* another two, my brothers' faces, in a father corner.

Orphelius, Henry, Kumiko, and Shelley—they are all gagged and chained. The women look as though they are not injured, but the seamen, my brothers, I see have been beaten.

Fuck. I regret that I'm excited—I don't see Athena down here. Hopefully, she's in better condition as I do believe Levi did have some affection for her.

"Put the clothes on!" shouts Levi as he points the gun in Henry's and Orphelius's direction.

I stand up doing as he says, pulling up trousers too short and a shirt too tight.

Don't they make clothes of my size in this time?

"Now turn around and clamp those chains around your wrists."

I turn around to see chains on the wall.

Levi growls. "Do it or I'll shoot both your friends in the legs."

Legs. As I clamp myself in chains, I recall that's all my brothers and I wanted. We thought about, cared about, talked about nothing else when we were first transformed.

Legs, I realize should've been the least important thing on our minds.

Freedom. Love. These are the things we had forsaken. These are the things it seems takes centuries for men to learn not to take for granted.

"Show me," demands Levi.

I turn around to show him I am bound.

"Great." He cocks a grin while keeping the gun pointed at the other seamen and pulls out a set of keys from his pocket. He tosses the keys at Kumiko. "Unlock your wrists."

She hesitates, so Levi aims the gun right at Orphelius's head.

"Do it, or I'll shoot the stupid octopus. It's time to go."

Orphelius is in protest, shouting with a muffle through his gag as he pulls at the chains on the wall. My friend is hurting himself, watching his lover do exactly as the demon demands. A vein on my friend's forehead looks as though it's about to pop as Kumiko gets up to leave to who knows where.

Henry cannot speak but the look on his face says everything as Shelley follows. Within moments, Levi has left with the girls, closing the door behind him and leaving a few other women to remain chained with me and my brothers in the dark.

13

ATHENA

My body shifts. To the right, I tip like a log, rolling just slightly and then onto my back and then to my left.

Creaking and knocking infiltrates my ears along with a swashing of some sort.

Where am I?

As I arouse, I realize I cannot open my eyes. I've been blindfolded. When I go to remove the blindfold, I notice my wrists are bound as well over my head. Quickly, I become alert—tugging—when I realize I'm on a bed...

A bed that sways.

A bed that must be on a ship.

A bed that I suspect belongs to a man Willis calls a demon.

My stomach twists. I'm in the demon's bed.

Thank heavens, I've been dressed. It's short and loose, feeling silky with spaghetti straps. What I'm wearing feels like a negligee, but at least I'm wearing something. I recall I was last naked with Willis before I was abducted from the sailboat.

Cries pierce through my ears along with heavy stomping aboard. The stomping and cries are coming closer. It sounds as if crying women are about to be led to where I am but they pass. They are led away, taken to another room it seems where their cries become muffled.

A latch clamors and I sense the door to the chamber I am in swing open.

Someone shuffles in and closes the door behind him. My ankle is grabbed by callused hands that I'm sure belong to man and I kick in a panic!

"Whoa, girl, calm down," an unfamiliar voice tries to soothe as my blindfold is removed. A finger is waved in front of me, too close to my eyes. "No damaging the goods," he chortles.

I blink, trying to gain focus on the face behind the taunting finger. I don't have my glasses and I'm not sure who he is until...

I think I recognize him.

And the patch over his eye confirms everything.

"How are you, Athena?" he smiles, bending to squat on the floor next to the bed to become eye level with me. "I've heard a lot about you." He taps on my nose and I wince. Instead, he puts out his hand as if he means to shake hands with me. "I'm not sure if you know me or not as we've never *formally* met."

Clearly, he can see that I'm tied up, so I can't shake hands and I grit my teeth when he laughs. *He's fucking with me.*

"I know who you are," I growl. "You're Bradley. Bradley Richmond. The poacher who took the baby dolphin from its mother and nearly killed the poor thing."

"Mmm," he smooths some of my hair out of my face and pulls out my glasses, putting them on for me. Once I realize I can see well, I go to kick him!

"Girl, I said whoa!" he steps back with a smirk as my legs fall off the bed and I roll over, hanging halfway off because my wrists are bound to the bed post.

I tug... *tug, tug, tug,* trying to get loose.

Whack! I'm smacked on the ass!

"Stop this now." Bradley grunts. "Stop it or I'll get upset and have to take it out on your girlfriends, maybe *all* the girls, in the next room."

"*All* the girls?" I question as I quickly pull myself back to the bed into the opposite corner.

"Kumiko and Shelley, they're both next door with two others. They're all being sold today." He smiles with a rub on his greasy chin. "Except for Kumiko, of course. She's mine." He winks. "Mine to torture. Along with her freak boyfriend."

Torture? My eyes get hot and watery, so I close them. I don't want this jerk to see me weak or crying, but I can't stop the wetness from springing.

"Oh, come now," coos Bradley in a gravelly tone. "What's happening to you and your girlfriends is hardly anything to fret over. There are worse things that could happen to you than being sold. Did you see what that fucking freak, Orphelius, did to me?" Bradley props his leg on the bed and pulls up the hem to show me his prosthetic leg. "That freak crushed my leg into millions of tiny pieces, pieces so small that even after I managed to swim ashore on the night we fought, doctors had to amputate up to my knee."

Bradley lifts his leg off the bed with the help of one hand and plants his leg on the floor. He grabs his hips, jutting his groin forward.

I should be laughing. He looks like a pirate. The patch, the stance, the crow's feet in the crook of his one good eye. *Oh, if only that leg were wooden!* Plus he's wearing faded slim black jeans adorned by a silver buckled black leather belt and a partially open, button-up tucked white collared shirt with sleeves rolled up to the elbow. Bradley looks exactly as though he were meant to play the part of a pirate. He even smells the part, putting off a rancid stench, like pig slop, making me believe he has not bathed or gone for a swim in days. His villainous appearance is quite comical really. But I'm not laughing. He just said I'm being sold.

"What about Willis?" I ask.

"You know, if you weren't worth so much, I'd beat you right now," he responds.

Beat me? I choke. Acid has risen to the top of my throat and I gag while trying hard to keep the bile back.

"Willis. I know he is one of those freaks. He and his friends—all *three* of them—will pay for what has happened to me, which reminds me..."

He leans over the bed, bringing his nose to nearly touch the tip of mine. His breath reeks. From what I'd previously heard of Bradley, he was a pretty, rich boy type, but it's obvious he's completely let himself go. Obsession, evil, revenge—I suspect those things make it easy for a man to rot from the inside out. The smell of his corrupt, decomposing soul is so thick, like a black fog made of pollution.

I cringe when he strokes the top of my head. "That's why I came in here. I wanted to thank you for everything, Athena. Without you, I wouldn't have been able to put all the clues together. The magical seamen—theirs is quite a tall tale, isn't it? But without hearing everything from you, Levi would've never learned the complete truth and reported back to me about it. I'm still not sure if Levi is a believer just yet in all this merfolk business, but don't worry." Bradley smacks my cheek lightly but the shame still stings. "I'll make sure Levi gets a front row seat when I harpoon your boyfriend and his mates. See, I've upgraded from dolphins to whales. It's all for sport, of course. I enjoy the hunt and although I do make money on whale meat, I've found my true trade is with women. I can't have your boyfriend and his crew of freaks getting in the way of my trade." Bradley dips his chin to get a better view of me—my *body*—so I turn my head away. "I'm sure you understand, Athena. Levi says you're quite the scholar. Too bad you don't need a brain where you're going."

My entire world begins to cave as Bradley exits. *Because of me! It's because of me! I'm the reason we've all been captured.* If I had not divulged on all those secrets and had done as my mother told since I was a child and kept my imagination to myself, Kumiko, Shelley, and I might not be in this mess. Not to mention, the only people who could've gotten us girls out of this would've been Willis and the other seamen.

I pull at the binds wrapped tight at my wrists but pause when I hear an engine approaching followed by screaming. It sounds like Shelley!

"Oi," says a gruff voice. It's a new voice, perhaps belonging to another crew member. "Let's go. Your new owner is here."

I tug harder at the binds. This can't be happening right now. Surely, this is just a nightmare and I need to wake up! Of course, I've read about maritime trade and the existence of slaves at various times in history. The sea is a vessel that makes human trafficking possible. One cannot seem to exist without the other.

Shelley screams again but she is quickly silenced and I clench my eyes shut. I want to scream for her but who will hear me? Once she goes missing she will never, *never* be heard from again. I wish there was a way to call for help, but how can I communicate an S.O.S?

A pang hits dead center in my chest.

The *dead*.

The magical dead can hear me.

I call out to Lenora, singing terribly.

Just as Shelley's Aunt Cora had once mentioned to me in passing when I was a teenager, I remember I should sing a sweet lament that goes quickly sour and off tune in hopes the lack of harmony will irritate the sea witch enough to...

"Athena," Lenora rattles. Her voice vibrates right at the outer edge of my ear canal.

I turn my head around, searching for the witch. I don't see her, but I feel her. Her presence looms like a haunting dark cloud but I'm grateful she's come to me.

"Lenora, we need help."

"Help?" she laughs, this time with a fading echo.

"Lenora, help us," I plead. "They're taking Shelley away."

"Mmm, yes. I see that. They're taking Kumiko to the other boat, too, it appears. I think they plan to have a party."

"If you see, then why don't you do something!"

Lenora laughs louder. "And what shall I do? Hmm, Athena?"

"Use your powers," I beg. "Get us out of here. Please! Before they become one of the missing forever."

"Maybe Shelley and a few others wouldn't be missing if you'd made those flyers sooner rather than later as the sheriff asked."

Shit! "I'm sorry. I really am."

"Well, of course, you're sorry now," Lenora scoffs. "You're about to become one of the missing, yourself, except you won't really be missing, will you? You know exactly where you're going."

"No," I shake my head.

"Sure, you do."

"No, I don't," I cry in denial although I know exactly where I'm headed...

To Hell.

"Lenora, please." I suck up my tears as the engine to a boat outside is revved. If I don't do something now, I know I'll never see the others again. "I want to make a trade."

"What!" shrieks the witch. "And I thought *you* were the smart one. It would seem as though you've learned nothing in your scholarly conquests."

"Will you trade with me or not?"

"Depends." She pauses. I wait. I think I can *hear* her contemplating. "What do you have to trade?"

I take a big breath and purse my lips to exhale slowly before I speak. "My life for Shelley's." I nod my head boldly. "A life for a li—"

"No," Lenora quickly cuts in. "That's not a good trade."

Not a good trade? How can she say I'm not a good trade? "What do you mean I'm not a good trade?"

"I mean, how will you pay? What can you give me in exchange for conjuring a spell to make such a swap? And what of the others? Are you just going to leave Kumiko to the pirate? You're not thinking properly, Athena. You are the Goddess of Wisdom. *Think* your way out of this."

I think. The truth is I'm so terrified, I have no idea how to use magic to get my way out of this mess.

But the witch...

She wouldn't be here if she didn't want something out of this situation as well.

"What do *you* want?" I ask her.

"I want Henry," she replies.

"Henry?" I'm baffled. "What in the world would you want with Henry?"

"I want him dead," replies Lenora. "I want a dagger pierced straight into his heart."

I shake my head. "No. There's no way."

"No way?" questions Lenora. "And what will Henry think when he finds out you let Shelley get taken. He would gladly trade his life for hers. All you'd have to do is kill him—*stab* him—when you get the chance after my deed in this plot is done."

"Kill Henry? I don't know that I could. And why Henry?" *It makes no sense.*

"Because I'm tired of listening to him." Lenora sighs. I can almost feel her invisible hot breath in my ear. "With Orphelius's powers came the ability to read minds of sea beasts. And there is no beast on this earth that sings a sadder song than Henry. Like a siren, he lures me in and I'm not equipped to help him with his physical ailments. But I can help him to cease with his laments."

The witch is right. Henry loves Shelley more than anything in all the world. I can't imagine how he would feel if he knew I let Shelley get taken when I could've saved her simply by trading his life for hers.

"And if I agree to ki... I mean, sta..." I swallow. I can't even say the words of the crime I must commit. "If I agree, what can you give me in return?" I cock my head towards the direction of the room where I know the other girls are being held. "How will you save *us*?"

"Truth be told, I can't *save* any of you," says Lenora.

"Yes, you can. You have magic," I remind her.

"No. I have the power to trick, trade, and transform and with that, I obtained the power of the storm and the power to control beasts. I can't use any of those powers on this ship. Everyone will drown. The women included."

"Then, why am I even talking to you!" I'm so frustrated.

"If you agree to this deal—one life in exchange for many," says Lenora, "I can set forth in motion the means for *all* of you to be rescued, to set everything right."

All of us? Rescued?

An inkling of hope sets in. "And how do you plan to *set forth* a rescue?"

"Oh, I don't know." Lenora is toying with me now. "Tell me, Athena. If you knew someone was in need of a rescue, what would *you* do?"

"I..." I can't think straight. "I honestly don't know."

"I'm calling the sheriff," she replies.

14

WILLIS

Feet suddenly shuffle above. The women begin whining, fearful of the captors that may be coming to take them... or hurt them.

"Shh." I try to quiet them so that I may listen to the feet moving about overhead in hopes I can map a layout of the space above. If I somehow end up getting out of these chains, the first thing I'll need to do after I free the others is head straight towards an exit.

The feet up top, however, seem to be stumbling but softly, as if the person walking about has no clue as to where to go. The feet pace forward and then back and then forward again but more slowly the second time around.

"Henry," mutters a gruff voice. "Orphelius."

Henry shakes his chains as Orphelius attempts to shout through the gag in his mouth. I take this as a sign. This must be a friend of theirs.

"We're down here!" I yell.

The feet move swiftly. They seem to be dancing now. The man upstairs is searching.

"We're underground!" I shout. "Look for the door."

A crack of light pierces through over the top of the stairwell but no one enters. All I see is the silhouette of a gun.

"This is the sheriff," the man announces. "Who's down there?"

"My name is Willis. There are others down here with me. We've been taken captive."

"Well, come on up," he growls. "But slowly. One by one."

"We can't sheriff." I jiggle my chains. "We are all tied up."

The sheriff shuffles about at the top of the landing until a light comes on. I see the tip of his gun aimed straight at me and then his eyes glaring from beyond. I show him my chains.

Satisfied I'm of no harm to him, he looks around. Taking notice of Henry and Orphelius in the corner, he puts his gun in his holster and skips down the steps.

"Jesus," he says when he sees two young, practically naked girls crouched as close as they can get together but barely touching one another as they are also gagged and chained.

The sheriff attempts to free the girls, but they cry with his failed attempts. They cry harder when he disappears up the stairwell, afraid he's left them. But the cries become screams of joy when the sheriff returns with a key, unlocking them both.

The lawman instructs the girls to head upstairs and outside where he says his deputy is waiting. The sheriff speaks into a black box and instructs the deputy to take the girls to the hospital. Taking a step towards the stairwell, it appears the sheriff plans to leave.

I shout, "Aye, what about us?"

The sheriff looks me over with a rub of his chin. "I don't know you." He looks over to Orphelius and Henry and points. "But I know them. Clearly, someone likes them a lot less than I do. Are you one of them? One of those *mer*freaks?"

I'm not sure what to say. I'd forgotten for a moment the

sheriff is the one who shot Henry. I shouldn't be surprised the sheriff would be content to just leave Henry and anyone like him down here. I need to say whatever I must to get myself out of these chains and get to Athena.

"No, I'm not."

"That's too bad," replies the sheriff as he hikes up the stairs.

My chest rises and falls quickly but heavily in a panic. *I can't believe the sheriff is going to leave us here!*

"Sheriff!" I shout towards the door he's left open. "Damn you. Let us out," I cry, yanking on the chains. "Shelley, Athena, Kumiko—they've been taken. They need our help. Come back here, you fucking bootlicker! If I was back to being that damn freak you hate so much, I'd fucking drown you." I come to standing, pulling at the chains, feeling the cold clamp of restraint at my wrists. "*SHERIIIIIF!*"

"Be quiet, you big oaf," he grumbles, careering down the stairwell. "Your locks are different from the girls. I had to get a different key."

He heads over to Orphelius, setting him free and then Henry. The sheriff continues to eyeball me suspiciously, looking up to me, as he unlocks my chains. "So, what's your superpower? You a fish? Or octopus, like the swordsman?" He chuckles. "Would be interesting if one of you was a shark. Hmm?" He raises a brow with a smirk, waiting for an answer.

I rub my freed wrists. "When I'm not human, I'm made of water."

"That's... uh..." The sheriff shakes his head. "*Not* very interesting. To think, I was just beginning to find your kind fascinating. This town, *my* town, has a way of always keeping me on my toes but then you had to go and bore me."

"I could wipe out your entire town as a single wall of water in the form of a tidal wave."

The sheriff gulps. "Like I said, *fascinating*."

Orphelius groans as he attempts to pick up Henry. Both the sheriff and I go over to help.

Once out of the building, which looks like an abandoned home, we all hop into the sheriff's mechanical carriage. I get in the back with Henry while Orphelius takes the front seat. We are all ears, curious as to how the sheriff discovered us. He says he got a tip from a random phone call.

We are also curious as to the sheriff's plan to rescue the girls, but when the sheriff says he can't use our help due to the danger of the situation, I give Orphelius a quick nod.

It feels good to be working with my sea mates again. As Orphelius grabs the wheel to steer and I headlock the sheriff from behind, it's Henry who is able to remove the sheriff's gun.

I suspect Henry and Orphelius feel the same as I do. These are just like old times and we are reveling in our abilities to overpower the sheriff, take over his carriage, and leave the lawman to curse us from the side of the road. Henry, however, is not thrilled to be holding the weapon that has crippled him, so he tosses the gun out of the window.

We agree to go to the marina. We need a fast ship with large sails and I recall seeing such a magnificent well-kept beauty in the bay.

Luckily, on arrival, the wind has picked up. Henry signals with his fingers overhead. I don't know the type of talk he makes with his hands, but I understand exactly what he's saying.

There's a storm coming.

Over the horizon, a few spirals of dark gray clouds loom low under a layer of fast—*speeding*—feathery clouds higher above. The atmosphere has gotten thick, despite the cool breeze blowing. Blue skies have disappeared, and lightning, it feels, could easily spark at any moment.

I look at the sea. Beyond the bay, waves are tumbling, rolling about in swells. I scratch my head. Now would *not* be a good time to take a boat out.

Orphelius gives me a hand to help Henry out of the car. I don't have to say in which direction we are going. The others have already spied the sailboat we have silently and without words agreed to steal.

Within minutes, I start the engine and we are at sea. With Henry seated at the helm, steering, as he'd always wanted for himself, Orphelius and I are quick to raise the sails and shut the engine off.

We sail straight into the horizon over rolling hills made of ocean waves and towards the flashing center of the storm. Like a sign, the storm beckons us and I know it is the sea witch who is helping us, showing us the way.

She needs me. Lenora needs me to rescue Athena so that the bargain Lenora and I struck will come to fruition granting the witch all three powers of the seas. I could not keep my powers for these two days. That was not part of the deal and I dare not think of what the witch will do once she possesses such magic. The power of the storm, the power of beasts, and the power to control water— it's unfathomable to think how she plans to use Poseidon's Trident. I only pray that once I get Athena back, Lenora does not intend to seek revenge and kill us all right away.

Up! Goes the bow of the boat and my stomach floats.

Yes! I feel as though we are flying.

Down! The bow crashes and I revel in the strength of my back, my thighs, and my knees absorbing all the energy of the sea.

The waves become taller as the wind on our backs blows with gusto into the sails. If my heart were not so consumed with impatience in getting Athena back, I daresay I would greatly be enjoying this. The sound of the wind—rumbling—

is music in my ears. And the smell of salted air, a scent I'd longed to sniff, makes me feel at home.

Water sprays in mists and globs as we crash straight ahead into wave after cresting wave. I turn to spy Henry up at the helm to make sure he is all right. He straightens his spine, giving me a salute and a wink. *Cocky capable bastard.*

I look to Orphelius, who's leaning over the edge and cheering. He claps his hands as one dolphin after another leaps into the air. It appears an entire family of oversized air-breathing fish is following us at our side.

"Friends of yours?" I shout.

"Ah, yes!" Orphelius shouts with a nod back.

"Perhaps you should tell them to get lost, especially the smaller one. There's only danger ahead."

"These creatures are no longer under my command. And if they were, I'd let them do as they please. Nothing pleases me more than to see them free."

Waves have managed to breach over the sides of the boat dropping a few small fish on the deck. Orphelius picks one up by its silvery tail and tosses the wiggler into the air.

Dolphins are apparently not the only creatures trailing us. A seagull with its own family in tow manages to catch and guzzle Orphelius's tossed fish down whole.

Rain falls now. Small, tiny drops splatter coolly over my arms.

I look once more towards the horizon and, in the distance, I see a black dot...

But it's a blur. Rain pours more heavily. Cold droplets are getting thicker as we get closer towards flashing lightning.

I take a breath. The last time the three of us decided to take on slavers, we nearly died and were transformed. I turn around to get a glimpse of my fellow seamen. They seem more eager than before to fight the battle ahead. Mystics, gods, monsters—it doesn't matter *who* or *what* you are—I would not want to be the entity keeping these men from the thing they cherish the most—the women they love.

I blink, wiping the rain away to get a better view of the horizon because I think I see two. *Two* dots. There are two boats out there.

The rain is battering down now as we get closer to the eye of the storm and I turn my head, searching, realizing we have nothing to mount an attack with.

I turn to my Master at Arms. "Orphelius, we have no weapons."

"Not to worry, Captain," he smirks. Orphelius bends down to pick up another fish and tosses it to his feathery friend.

Is he mad? We are making our approach and he's feeding the damn bird above!

I recognize it's been a while (give or take a few hundred years) since we've plundered. Like pirates, we've behaved together in the past, but we almost always had a plan. *Almost.* We did, however, *always* have weapons.

"Orphelius!"

He shakes his head unbuttoning his shirt, with a shout towards the helm. "Henry," Orphelius calls. "I'm going overboard."

Henry waves his hands before he pulls up his own shirt.

"Oh no," replies Orphelius, pointing. "You're not coming. You're staying right there. You are not allowed to transform. You know what the doctors have said. If that bullet in your back moves in the slightest…"

Henry scoots off his chair to land flat on the deck.

"Captain, tell him!" cries Orphelius. "Tell Henry he can't—"

With one pull up and a bellying tip over the edge of our ship, Henry disappears.

I scurry to peep over the side. Between the rain and the rough waves, I can hardly see a thing until...

I'm fairly confident I just saw a seaman with a damn fishtail.

"Well," says a naked Orphelius. "I think you'll need more weapons. Don't you?"

"Aye," I groan and sigh when my Master at Arms also jumps overboard.

A wave crashes port side nearly tipping over my boat. As much as I wish I could jump in with the other seamen, unlike them, I would not transform. In fact, I'd probably drown. I'm stuck, by my bargain, in this human form until sunrise.

Quickly, I make my way up to the helm and take hold, steering myself towards the ship I suspect is holding Athena and must belong to that demon.

His ship, a rusted black mass of thick tin, is ten times the size of my boat.

Drifting across his starboard side, I notice there are a few men on board. I see the men are all lined up...

Lined up with guns...

And those guns are all aimed right at me.

15

ATHENA

Gunshots. The pace of my pulse quickens as what sounds like gunshots ring out.

I tug at the ropes that bind my wrists to the bed.

More gunshots go off. Like fireworks, they fire off repeatedly except now more sporadically and in the company of screaming.

Are those men *screaming?*

I figure the witch did as she said she would, following through on her part of the bargain and informing the sheriff of our whereabouts. I only hope the sheriff also called for help and brought a task force of some kind. Only he and the deputy plus a few retired police volunteers are responsible for our small town. What Bradley has going on here is undoubtedly part of some larger crime syndicate and, although I've never heard the sound of an automatic weapon before, I'm well aware of the type of effort and organization it must take to obtain weapons like the ones I'm sure are sounding off right now.

And it sounds like there are dozens of them shooting off

outside of this room. It sounds like there's a war going on out there.

What the hell are they firing at?

"Get the girls!" shouts Bradley approaching from outside. "We need bait."

My door unhinges, revealing a very pissed off pirate with a huge gun strapped over his shoulder.

"Let's go," he commands, pulling a knife from his back pocket.

My body tenses as he steps forward and begins to cut at my binds.

I'm not sure what to do. *Should I be fighting him? Or should I let him cut me free in hopes I can overpower him and attempt an escape later?*

The glimmer of the blade sawing near my wrists feels as torturous as being bound. I remember thinking once when I'd learned about what happened between Kumiko and Bradley, why she didn't fight back harder against him. I remember thinking that I would've easily fought back if someone had tried to force themselves upon *me*. But right now, with this… this man with a gun and blade plus a stench so strong he smells worse than death—I feel paralyzed.

Bradley catches my eye as he cuts and gives me a devilish up-quirk of a side smirk.

I pout, helpless in my own skin.

Levi might be a demon, but this man, Bradley Richmond, is the Devil, and he knows exactly the power he has over me right now.

"You gonna come nicely?" The Devil asks. "Or do I have to drag you out by your heels to meet your freak?"

My freak? Willis is here? This is why the men are screaming outside. I suspect Willis is not alone.

I swing my legs around feeling more confident about the situation even though I know there are bullets flying about.

Even though I'm doing exactly as the Devil asks and heading towards the door, Bradley still decides to push me. I land on the floor face-down.

Turning around, rolling over to my back, I look at the man standing straddled above me and chortling. He points his gun down at me. "You do as I say when we get out there. Do you understand, Athena?"

I don't say anything. There's an itch, an overwhelming urge to try to escape, especially knowing that Willis is out there.

My thoughts betray my face and Bradley kicks me in my side, which is shocking!

I clam up. The immediate sting to my ribs isn't too bad but I know it's going to bruise later.

"Now look what you made me do," he scowls. "Do you think your new owner is gonna want you when you're all bruised up?" Bradley flicks his greasy blond locks back.

"Maybe I should tie you back up. I can see why Levi likes you so much." He licks his lips. "You're too smart for your own good. Perhaps you're not ready for sale. Perhaps you need a few whips to teach you subjection. Hmm?" He kicks me again. "Do you need a lesson in understanding your place?"

There are too many loose screws in Bradley's head. Above deck, there are guns firing, people screaming, and a storm raging, but this loony is finding it necessary to take a timeout from the havoc outside to teach me a lesson in slavery.

Bradley's towering over me, but I'm confident if I just lift my leg and kick really hard, kick him in his balls! I could probably render him helpless.

Or maybe not.

Reluctantly, the words, "I know my place," flow from my quivering lips.

"Good. Get up. And get on deck."

I roll over to my knees and get up, reaching for the door handle. Upon opening the door, I see another armed man waiting.

"Take her," Bradley says as the other man fists my hair at the back of my head, yanking me and then pushing me forward.

The man places the tip of his gun hard into my back as we get to a metal staircase. Hiking up the steps, I see a door.

"Go." The man digs his gun more firmly into the soft right flank of my back. Right where Bradley kicked me! So, I swiftly move my feet to avoid the pain.

Opening the door, I squeal as lightning flashes furiously before my very eyes.

"Go!" The man yells, again digging his gun painfully into my side.

Within milliseconds I am drenched as I step out onto the deck. It is taking every bit of effort to keep myself from slipping. My bare feet can barely keep me stabilized with all the rain spurting and pooling about.

Every inch of my body is being struck by rain. I shiver as icy cold wet drops pierce every point of my body, in the corners of my eyes, and even going up my nose. A strong whirlwind wraps itself around me nearly knocking me over, but I'm grabbed.

I wiggle as the claws of the armed man manage to grip right under my armpit. He digs and I squirm in reaction.

To both of our surprise, I somehow manage to free myself from him, standing more than a few feet away. Like a bull, his nose flares and just as some of the sailors are doing around me, I decide to *run* as he charges.

I don't know why I'm running. I'm on a teetering ship in the middle of the ocean. I have no idea where I'm supposed to go and certainly not overboard. I see there are twenty-foot waves waiting to pummel and drown me.

LOVERS IN DEEP

The ship tilts and, of course, I slip. The next thing I know, I'm on my knees again. I'm grabbed by the shoulder and smacked in the face with a backhand.

Ugh! I grab my head to calm the dizzying effect.

"Why you fucking cunt!" the man blares, raising his hand once more.

I shut my eyes, readying to take another backhand...

But...

It doesn't come...

I hear a yelp and squint open one eye.

The man is gone.

I turn my head around, searching for a sign of him when I hear another yelp and words which sound like "help." The words are coming from beyond the ship.

Helping myself up, I grab the ship's rails, daring myself to look overboard.

Through the blurring rain, I see the man who hit me outside of the ship and treading water ferociously among turbulent surf and squalls. His eyes are so wide, he looks desperate. "Help me!" he yells.

From a few feet beyond the man screaming, I swear I just saw something... the flick of a very large tail fin, although I'm not entirely sure.

It seems my captor also saw what's coming for him and he shouts for help even louder. The ship teeters and the man is screaming now.

I make eye contact with my former captor and watch as two separate hands reach up out of nowhere to quickly pull my captor under where he disappears into an angry black sea.

I crouch. Planting my butt on the floor and my back against the inner wall of the ship, I hug my knees to my chest. I'm not exactly sure how, but I suspect Henry somehow leaped out of the water to nab my captor and took him overboard.

A pain thickens inside me. The witch tricked me. She said she would put into motion the means to free us by calling the sheriff. But all she did was tell the sheriff where the seamen were and now they are here.

I clasp my hands to my mouth to hide the scream that escapes me and the horror that I can't believe I hadn't noticed yet, the horror unfolding before my very eyes.

Tentacles are reaching over the opposite edge of the ship plucking captors one by one to either be tossed into the storm or suffocated and crushed.

The horror of what I must do is beginning to eat away at me. In exchange for all of *this*, I have to kill Henry.

Bradley appears strolling past me with such confidence, he is completely unfazed by the sea monsters wreaking havoc on the last remaining members of his crew. Bradley heads straight towards the apex of the front deck, towards a huge mechanism I also had not noticed earlier—an oversized harpoon gun.

The harpoon gun is bolted into a raised platform at the bow. It looks like an enormous gun—a *whale* killer—that is three times a man's size. As rain continues to batter over our heads, Bradley appears to be loading the harpoon, setting it up to shoot. He swings the harpoon around, aiming it straight over the ship's edge, pointing into the sea.

From the corner of my eye, I see Orphelius's tentacles retract and the ship rolls but that does not distract Bradley from keeping his grip on the trigger.

Suddenly, a siren blares and a voice, the sheriff's voice, speaks loudly through what seems to be speakers. "Hold there!" Pike says through a megaphone. "This is the sheriff's department."

"You have no jurisdiction out here," shouts back Bradley.

As I muster the courage to get on my knees and peep over the rails, I see the waves and rain are calming. I've never been more elated to see the sheriff's blue and red flashing lights.

"Errr." I also see Levi. He's cuffed along with another, much older man—Shelley's buyer?—on a smaller vessel. Thankfully, Levi's been caught and I pray he goes to prison.

"I have jurisdiction if I believe you're trafficking women. Step away from your weapon," demands the sheriff, pulling out his handgun. "Step away and prepare for me to come on board."

"Step away?" Bradley says and a billowing laugh escapes his lips. "Do you have any idea what's out here? What's lurking beneath your boat?"

"Aye, he has a good enough idea." My heart leaps out of my chest when I see Willis, *beautiful* Willis, coming out from behind the cabin to stand next to the sheriff.

My insides do a somersault when I also see Kumiko and Shelley peek out of the cabin windows. They've already been rescued!

"Aargh," grunts an infuriated Bradley. "I don't know how you freaks managed to get free, but *that* one." He points to Kumiko. "That little witch belongs to *me*," he yells, spinning the harpoon gun and firing in her direction.

The harpoon shoots through the air but is deflected, shredding through one of Orphelius's elongated arms. Orphelius is successful but hurt and thankfully not dead, which only seems to infuriate Bradley more.

The pirate pulls the gun strapped over his shoulder forward and begins firing. The sheriff fires back and the two become caught up in a shootout.

Everyone is screaming all over again. And me? I'm crouched, covering the lenses of my glasses because I have no idea what to do when...

The shooting stops.

"Henry!" cries Shelley.

I peep my head over the rails again to see Willis dive into the sea.

All is quiet.

Even the waves calm into a soft roll.

Everyone aboard the sheriff's boat is waiting in suspense.

Everyone aboard the ship I'm on is dead. Bradley included. The sheriff must've got him.

Willis finally rises to the surface and he's not alone. In his arm, rests his friend, Henry, who does not seem to be moving. Not even breathing.

16

WILLIS

Red. That's all I see.

Gripping my friend in my arms, I take a quick second to look behind me, towards the horizon to see the sun is setting where the sky is also red and orange. The once damp clouds look as though they have been set on fire.

When I peer back at my paling fish friend, however, I recognize the sea, itself, is a much *deeper* red at where I am keeping us afloat. He's been shot. He's bleeding out.

"Bring him," says the sheriff, reaching out his hand.

I look the sheriff in the eyes but I can't see his irises. His oversized darkened spectacles are covering half his face. I have no idea if I can truly trust the lawman.

Yes, the sheriff plucked me out of the sea when I had no choice but to jump overboard before I was shot by Bradley's men. But, and this is a *big* but, the sheriff is the one responsible for the fact that Henry can't walk.

The sheriff tosses his glasses and stretches his hand further towards Henry. "Captain," the sheriff says to me. "You can trust me. I'm a believer now."

Hauling Henry over to the sheriff because I have no choice, "In merfolk and magic?" I ask.

"No," the sheriff replies. "In the *people* of my town."

I nod, placing my friend in the sheriff's hands.

Shelley is beside herself, crying. Kumiko is doing her best to console Shelley and prevent her from diving in as the sheriff and I struggle to hoist the half man, half oversized fish onto the boat. Orphelius joins us, although he struggles as well.

Orphelius, it appears, was not only hit by the harpoon but is harboring multiple gunshot wounds. Thankfully, his injuries are nowhere in his torso. Only in each of his eight limbs. And I'm sure they hurt.

Once onboard, I stammer to kneel at Henry's side. Despite Shelley's attempts to wake the seaman, Henry remains unconscious.

A swarm of emotions flurries within me. After everything my mates and I have been through, *this* is how Henry's story ends?

Henry was a fine man... *is* a fine man. Surely, he is a much finer, more honorable man than I. I think of where he came from—at the end of the line—and where he wanted to be— always at the forefront of whatever vocation he took on.

It doesn't matter what form Henry takes. Whether he is a man or a monster, a lover or a fighter, Henry takes all things in stride and never gives up.

A salty tear falls from my eye to land in my mouth. I can't give up on him now.

"Lenora," I cry out to the sea witch. I know she is near. The lightning and the rain have ceased but there are dark clouds directly above, looming as if they are watching.

"Lenora!" I stand with a shout, turning towards the deepest darkest part I can see of the sea which happens to be directly under us.

A head pops up. "Stop shouting and stop crying." The dark-skinned head of the sea witch draped in seaweed cocks from left to right. She's studying me. "Women's wailing is like music to the gods, but a man crying..." She offers a smirk. "Especially a man of your size and strength... bluh." She pokes her tongue out.

"Help him!" Shelley flicks her red hair out of her face before she crawls through Henry's blood diluted by seawater spreading across the deck. Shelley reaches the edge where she hangs over, pleading. "Please, Lenora. I'll do anything. Give you whatever you want. Bring Henry back."

Henry makes a gurgling sound and we all turn to see the merman struggling to breathe as the gills at his chest come open and close while his nose also flares. Warily, his eyes open as he reaches out to Shelley, who is immediately back at his side.

"Looks like he's not quite dead yet," Lenora says, spinning her head around with a quick glance back at Bradley's ship.

I follow Lenora's gaze. Athena is standing port side with two other girls, who I assume are other former captives, watching. If I could go to her, I would. I wish to take Athena in my arms and embrace her but now is not the time.

"Help him," I tell Lenora. "Help Henry before he dies."

"I can't help him," the witch rattles. "I already have his powers and there's nothing else he can trade that I need."

"Damn you, witch!" I curse. "Can't you just help him? For *once*, can't you just—"

"Magic doesn't work that way," Lenora interjects. "I cannot create something out of nothing or make something happen without a trade."

I close my eyes and take a breath before I spit out the only trade I can make. "Take my life. Mine for Henry's."

"No!" screams Athena from the top of her lungs and to my surprise, she is not the only one in disagreement.

Shelley grabs at my hand. "No, Henry doesn't want that. Look. Look at him."

Henry is indeed shaking his head. It's a small gesture, and I'm thankful he's alert but I'm his Captain and I will do as I see fit.

The witch, however, likewise shakes her head. "I'm not trading your life for Henry's. You must complete your end of our bargain, *but*..."

But? Henry gurgles again. The man is dying! *Slowly.* He's leaking as well as choking on his own blood and I can't believe we are taking our sweet time having this conversation!

"What is it!"

"I could trade one bargain for another."

"What do you mean?"

"I could swap out the details between two bargains I've already made." The witch is smiling bigger than I've ever seen before.

"Whatever it is, I'll do it," I say. I don't need to hear the details. Henry's life depends on a trade.

"Are you willing to die at the hand of your lover?" The witch pokes her thumb up to Athena.

"Excuse me?" I ask, looking across the narrowing space that rests between our boat and the ship atop which Athena stands. She and I make eye contact but Athena breaks the bond by covering her face with her palms.

Dark thoughts enter my mind. Athena has made her own trade and I put the pieces together. Athena is the reason the sheriff found us. But a lot of this is not Athena's fault. The witch works mysteriously and to what aim? No one knows.

"What did Athena trade?" I'm afraid to ask.

"Henry's life," the witch replies.

"What!" Shelley fires.

"Be quiet, flamethrower," says Lenora as thunder booms

overhead. "Athena traded Henry to save many. Athena's only task was to take Henry's life, but it looks as though fate is about to let Athena off easy by letting Henry die of his own free will."

"No," Shelley cries, bending over to plant her head in Henry's chest.

"There is a workaround." Lenora pops her shoulders up above the surface and we all perk up.

"What is that?" I ask.

"The bargain that you and I struck expires at sunrise. Will your power to control the seas to me *now* and I will save Henry."

My heart beats alternating in rhythm between feelings of joy and feelings of dismay. "And what do you want in return?"

Lenora glides closer to the boat. "A life is still owed by morning. Rather than Henry, Athena must take *your* life, the life of her lover, instead."

I hesitate, though I shouldn't. Henry is on the brink! But Athena... is it possible she could kill me on command? She's not a seaman or a soldier. "And what if she can't do it?" I ask. "What if Athena chooses not to kill me. Then what?"

"You'll have to make sure that she does," replies Lenora. "Or I will have to come to collect her. Her *soul*." More thunder echoes. "So, what will it be, Captain? Your life for Henry's life? Will your powers to me now and everyone will remain alive and free. I'll even let you keep your eyes since you won't need them once you're dead come morning."

"Done."

"Willis, no!" wails Athena but it's beyond her control. The bargain is struck.

Lenora's head disappears, dunking beneath the surface but I don't try to keep her in my sights. Henry is making the most uncomfortable noises. When I look to him, his whole body is buckling as he chokes on his own blood and I kneel at his side.

Thunder cracks overhead but not one of us dares to look above. For all we know, the witch could be lying. I've already lost claim to the powers once granted to me. I have no idea if the witch truly intends to save Henry or not as this could simply be another one of her tricks.

Henry still looks as if he's dying. His skin is paling. His scales are wrinkling. We all huddle close to him. Even the sheriff has taken a knee.

The boat sways and the seagulls flying overhead begin to caw. In a screeching chorus, the birds cry louder and louder until we all find ourselves looking up to the sky at the cause of the commotion.

Swirling overhead, the clouds are beginning to spin. Faster and faster, they twirl as our boat gets knocked by a wave. I grab onto Kumiko who nearly falls over.

As the boat gets knocked again I look to the sea and lo and behold a woman's head, a head shaped by water and the size of a barge, is rising from the depths.

Water splashes from every direction and begins to shower, pouring from above. With the powers I've granted, Lenora stands to become a monstrosity. She is the size of a mountain hovering over the boat. The crown of her head nearly touches the clouds to where she reaches, spinning her hand made of seawater and pulling what appears to be a bolt of lightning.

The air between the group of us begins to move. It's gentle at first but gusts blow. The wind picks up and we are all finding it difficult to stay put. We are in a whirlwind gasping for air.

"Lenora!" I cry out as the wind, spinning violently, pushes us all away from Henry. The wind is so strong it feels as though it is about to pick us up and toss us overboard when...

Henry is lifted. In a funnel, like a cyclone, the merman rises, levitating to a magnificent height. Blood is allowed to drain from him, getting caught up in the whirlwind spinning around him.

"Lenora!" I screech. *She said she would save him! She's killing him!*

A fine stream of water shoots up out of the sea. The single stream arches over us, shooting into the top of the funnel and appears to pierce Henry's wounded flesh. Lightning held in the giant hand of the witch comes to a fine point and also cuts through the merman.

The light is so bright I reluctantly look away. I can hear the others, especially Shelley, calling Henry's name. When I look back briefly, I see Lenora has completely opened Henry up. At both the front and the back, she has spliced the man —*gutted him! Like a fish!* From his waist up to his neck, I see his innards. His own blood is still spinning around him. And he is becoming increasingly more aware. *My poor friend!* His eyes are rolling, and his tail is twitching.

Be still Henry, says Lenora, forcing the merman to become motionless with her power to control sea beasts. I find it strange hearing her speak to him in my mind.

Lenora finally appears to be closing Henry's wounds, except he seems to be choking again. The slits—his gills—on his chest come to a close and his fin begins to shrivel.

He's transforming.

Henry's tail splits down the middle to become legs as he is lowered, planted face down on the deck.

All the blood once encircling him has been returned to him. I see no sign that Henry is in any danger. I see only scars.

And legs.

And breathing.

The clouds disperse as Lenora quickly reshapes herself

into a human form to stand among us. Walking her bare feet towards Henry, she stands, hovering—admiring her handiwork.

"How do you feel?" she asks as the rest of us remain silent and in awe.

Henry takes a long breath, coming up on one hand and his knees. The fist he's been making comes open and my heart soars when I see a bullet in his palm.

Could it be? Is that the bullet that was in his back?

The sheriff topples over, falling onto his arse. I suspect he is happy considering the look of bewildering relief on his face.

Lenora seems proud. "Well," she says to Henry. "Do you have anything to say?"

Henry cocks his head up, searching. His head spins but stops when he sees Shelley.

"I love you," he says exasperated with a smile.

Shelley wails and she is instantly in front of him, kissing him, grabbing him, holding him, groping him...

The witch appears to be irritated as she sighs. "I meant to me," she interrupts their magical moment. "Don't you have anything to say to *me*?"

Shelley reluctantly lets go of Henry as he pushes his lover away so that he may come to standing. He turns with a slight wobble and walks to Lenora to give her a big hug. "Thank you."

"You're welcome."

Henry squeezes Lenora tighter. "I've been wishing to speak again so badly but I have no idea what to say to you to express my gratitude."

Lenora forces a cough. "That's enough. You're naked. It's uncomfortable that you're holding me naked and your woman is watching anyway."

Henry laughs, letting go to get wrapped back up in Shelley's arms again.

Of course, I am overjoyed at this moment but as the sun slips below the horizon, joy seems to be going with it.

I turn my head to see Athena on the ship across the way.

She too slips.

She ducks her head down to hide behind the ship's rails where I can no longer see her.

As a boy, I remember wondering where the sun went when it sunk. I wondered what treasures lay guarded by monsters in the deep beyond. My curiosity was the reason I became a seaman.

As Lenora slips back into her ocean domain and the sheriff starts up the boat's engine so that we may collect the others, I take a moment to consider my final plot. I have one last night left to live and, in this night, I must convince my lover to send me to where the sun shall never rise again.

Athena *must* kill me.

If she doesn't, she will lose her soul and I could never live with myself knowing she would be lost to oblivion for eternity.

I'm not that kind of man or a monster.

17

ATHENA

I can't do it.
 I won't.
I refuse to kill Willis.

I should've taken all that treasure he lay at my feet and ran with it! To think, I could be sunbathing poolside atop my million-dollar deck alongside my million-dollar mansion on a white sanded coast while listening to Lady Gaga and being served by my hot pool guy named Alejandro.

I plant my butt on my bed and drop my face in my hands. The sheriff was nice enough to drop me off at home after we left the other girls at the hospital. I could tell he also wanted to talk, to clarify his understanding of everything that happened earlier. Pike did most of the talking and he seemed to understand the complexity of the situation, which all boils down to the fact that I either kill Willis or end up without my soul.

The sheriff, however, doesn't seem worried in the least with the possibility that I might commit *murder*. As he walked me up the staircase to my door, he said there was no way I'd ever kill anyone. Sure, I helped bust Henry out of jail but the sheriff claimed he knew I was not the type who could ever take another's life. Of course, that didn't stop him from separating Willis and I *and* also inspecting my apartment *and* taking every knife and sharp object that could be used as a weapon when he left.

Pike also put the deputy on overnight duty, ordering his subordinate to keep watch at the beach house where the others were left to also monitor Willis, whom the sheriff placed under house arrest.

I lay down, plopping the back of my head firm into my super soft pillow and rubbing my forehead. I begin to wonder what Hell is going to be like. Because I'm sure that's where my soul is going...

To *Hell*.

Maybe it's not that bad. It can't be worse than this. All this anxiety pent up...

...the anticipation...

...the waiting...

My conscious is already on fire. It's driving me crazy! I wonder if I should head over to the beach to get it over with and let Lenora take me now.

There's a knock at the door. Well, it's not really a knock. It sounds like Pike's close-fisted pound-on-wood routine.

Of course! I'm contemplating the line between life and death, Heaven and Hell as my soul is at stake and Pike still needs something from me.

I plant my fists at my side. "What do you want?"

"Open the door," says a low gravelly voice, which makes me tuck my head under the pillow.

I don't say anything. Maybe if I manage to keep quiet long enough, Willis will just go away.

"Athena," he shouts. "Open the door before I break it down."

I look at the hinges, the doorknob, and the bolt. Everything looks strong and intact. If it's made to keep out burglars, I'm sure the hardware can keep out the tough guy who's survived magic, a shootout, and an era before antibiotics.

Willis wiggles the doorknob and pounds with a heavier fist this time. "Athena!"

I swing my legs out of the bed. He just shook the whole building, making my knick-knacks of seashells and sea glass chime with a warning. The building is old, built in the 1800s. I trust the hinges, but I'm not so sure I can trust the building's infrastructure.

Walking up to the door, I speak through the crack. "What do you want?"

I know what he wants. He wants me to kill *him.*

Not. Happening.

"Let me in," he says. I can tell he's leaned his mouth against the opposite side of the crack as well.

"How did you get here? The sheriff says you weren't supposed to leave the beach house until he could collect more details for his case. He's going to have to come up with a story for all those dead bodies that doesn't include monsters. He gave you specific instructions to stay put. You're supposed to be under house arrest."

Willis laughs haughtily. "Come now. The deputy was no match for my mates and me, and the sheriff still judges us poorly. Why in the world the sheriff would think Henry and Orphelius would take orders from a lawman is quite baffling. My mates still consider me their captain. They only take orders from me. Now..." He wiggles the knob. "Do as I say and open the door."

"You're not *my* captain. I don't take orders from you."

"Damn, girl," he curses. "You're making me angry."

"I don't care if you're angry and I'm not a girl, so don't talk down to me. Now go away."

"Athena, open. Don't make this harder than it has to be."

A pang hits my chest and my eyes water. "I can't do it," I say, leaning into the door. "Please let me spend my last few hours in peace and go away."

His voice vibrates through me from the opposite side of the wood slab. "I don't understand. You were willing to trade Henry—take *his* life—to save the others, but you won't take mine to save yourself."

Willis has me all wrong. Like the sheriff said, I'm not a killer.

I bow my head. My eyes are getting hot. "I would never have hurt Henry." I wipe the tear away that runs down my cheek.

I think back. I'm not exactly sure that I even agreed to the bargain and the mess I'm in now. I did not *verbally* say anything. The witch said she was going to call the sheriff and then she was gone. I admit, however, that I was relieved knowing she was going to get help, and I did not call out to stop her.

"So, was it your intention all along to fall short on your end of the bargain?" Willis asks. "You, the scholar, should know you can't mess with magic like that. You should've known you'd have to follow through."

"I would never hurt Henry," I repeat myself. "I could never hurt *you*."

"Then open the door for me, Athena. I'm aching to be with you right now. In all my years, not for centuries, have I ever hurt so badly. Appease me. Let me in. Let me hold you until your time comes."

I suck up a sniffle. He *hurts*, he says. That was the last thing I would've ever wanted for him. I open the door.

A big sigh blows from the pouty lips coming into view. I don't even get to look Willis in the eye before his large hand is pushing on the door, forcing me to step back. The next thing I know, those pouty lips are all over me. They press

LOVERS IN DEEP

into my mouth as big biceps wrap around my shoulders, squeezing and lifting me from the floor. My feet dangle as Willis, a mass of solid muscle, moves us both backward and I'm thrown.

I land flat on my back on my bed and I quickly sit up, leaning on my hands. I want to resist this. I want to resist *him*. I know what he's doing. He thinks he's going to make love to me and seduce me and get me to bend to the power of his will and do what he asks. But it's not going to happen. I need to resist him because it will be easier to let go. Let *him* go. He is not going to get me to...

He takes off his shirt. Every fine muscle over his ribs and abdomen is rippling as he breathes. He's breathing so heavy.

He unbuttons his fly. The zipper comes down and I feel hot, ashamed, because I can't keep my eyes from turning away.

His erection springs out as he drops his pants and I blush. I remember the thick, elongated mysterious mass that has an upward curve.

I recall the first time I saw his length while we were on the boat and I'm still intrigued. *Is that how it's supposed to be? I thought those things were supposed to be straight. That thing* still *looks like it's made to gut and carve me from the inside out.*

Willis wraps one hand around the front of his shaft and fists himself. He rakes his bleached hair back from his eyes with his other set of fingers.

He's staring at me now. Our eyes are locked as he strokes himself.

Willis, the man once made of water, seems to be preparing himself, checking to be sure his weapon is fully pumped, hard, and ready to take on its next great conquest.

Me.

"Willis," I mumble, scooting back.

He smiles cockily as he releases himself. He stands up straighter and looks me over before he climbs over me.

The mattress tips back and forth as his thick thighs and heavy knees plow into the bed.

"Remove all of this, Athena," he says, tugging at my pajama top before he comes to hover above me.

"I'm not remov—"

He kisses me. His body lands heavily against mine and I find that I am sinking deep into the mattress. Willis's breath is hot, but it tastes and smells sweet, like citrus. Like he crushed a couple of mandarins earlier between those perfect pearly white canines of his.

He withdraws, licking his lips, leaving my taste buds dressed in tangy fruit. "Athena," he repeats, placing the tip of his nose on mine while sliding his hand up my thigh and through my loose cotton pajama shorts.

"Yeah," I answer, dizzy, as his fingers trail towards my crease.

"Take off your clothes."

"I..." I close my eyes. This feels like a dream. One I've had over and over again except this time I can actually *feel* something real and I'm rejoicing. *This is my dream come true!*

Willis's hand has made its way beneath the tight layers of cotton I'm wearing and he's stroking his calloused fingers along that most smooth, sensitive flesh of my inner slit. The sensation is both exciting and calming, tickling and electrifying, and out of nowhere, I'm...

Wet.

His finger slips into me.

I gasp, ready to screech, but a nibble on my lip followed by a thrust of a slippery tongue penetrating my mouth keeps me silent.

Willis's finger continues to penetrate me. In and out he works when suddenly he has unhooked his finger from within me and is flicking, teasing at my clit, and then rubbing. Circularly. I can't catch my breath.

"Wil-lis," I murmur, escaping his mouth, but keeping my face close to his to inhale him deeply as he breathes me in as well.

He rubs harder, fiercer, before his fingers take another plunge.

I'm moaning, so he repeats this cycle. Plunging and then rubbing.

An urge inside of me quickens. I feel as though I'm on the edge. I've been caught and placed on the edge of something sharp and I want to be cut free. I want to come. *Oh God, I'm so close!* So close to...

He withdraws.

I clutch at Willis's arms, his massive, swollen beefy arms. "No, don't stop!" I beg, flipping my eyes open to see his wicked gaze.

"Remove your clothing," he commands, and I quickly attempt to pull everything off.

Moments ago, I was embarrassed of being so vulnerable even though he's seen me completely naked before. But now, I can't wait to have him touch me. Have his way with me.

I slow down when I realize he's watching, his arms and legs spread, hovering over me. His breath hitches when my breasts come free and he lifts an arm to tug on his cock as I wiggle to remove my bottoms.

When I'm completely naked, he comes up on his knees, lifts and grabs my thighs, and then yanks! Pulling my body towards him.

"Oh, Captain," I say as he glides the heated head of his cock up and down along the inner folds of my silken slit.

Willis's smile turns devious as he spreads my legs wide, taking one last good look before he aims the tip of his thick curve at my entrance. He makes eye contact with me and impales me.

He buries himself inside me. Each hard thrust of his raking curve feels as though he is trying to dig his way deeper and deeper within me.

He's going hard. I've never done this before, but I know he's going hard on me.

And I take it. I take every hard inch of his hook because I want it. I want him. I want this man. I always have. He saved me and I'll save him. We were always meant to be like this and end this way. He was mine from the start and no matter where I go or what I become, his memory will be mine for all eternity.

"You like that, Athena?" He slams into me repeatedly, thinking he can fuck me and make me feel indifferent towards him—*hate* him.

He's mad if he thinks that could ever happen.

"Yes, Captain," I reply because I like this. I like him. He's difficult to handle. He's so big and so intense. I sense that at any moment he's going to break me. I just bite my lip and grip my pillows enjoying every bit of the strength and power he has.

With a grumble, he grips at my hips, pulling me over the full length of his shaft and pumps me hard with every ounce of energy that his working muscles could exhaust. The slapping of our bodies echoes in harmony with the rattling of the walls. *This man sure knows how to make a lot of noise.*

"You want it more like this?"

"Please, Captain," I beg as my body is jerked wildly in his grasp.

He groans as he thrusts even harder and something in me shifts. Once more, I'm at the crest! My body tenses. *Oh my, I'm going to co...*

"No." Willis pulls out.

Something within me breaks. I'm at a loss. *I was on the brink!* I was at the edge of the horizon, ready to slip past the edge of the earth to fall and float within a great void that I know could only come from an orgasm.

"Willis!" I snap.

He comes off the bed, reaching for his pants and pulling them on. "This is wrong. This is not how this should be."

I'm so angry. *Furious!*

But he looks so solemn. Sad.

My heart breaks. "Willis?"

He sighs, pulling over his shirt.

I reach for my own clothes. "*What's* wrong? Did I do something wrong?"

"There is nothing wrong and yet everything is wrong," he says, helping me to put my shirt over my head.

Wrong. Wrong. That's all I hear. And I know he's talking about me. Again, I feel like that stupid little girl in love since she could remember with a creature that could never love her back because we are from two different worlds except that he is not the monster—I am.

"What is wrong with me that you don't want me?" I'm ready for Lenora to take me to Hell *now*.

"Oh, Athena," he sits next to me and strokes my hair away from my face before he cups my cheeks and kisses my forehead. He pulls a knife from his back pocket. It's small. I hadn't noticed it in his pants earlier.

He puts the handle in my palm.

I cringe, shaking my head. We went straight from love making to *murder*. "No."

"Yes," he says, clasping my hand around the handle and guiding the knife's point to his ribs.

"No, stop!" I screech. We are each struggling to fight against the other.

He is so strong. "You must do this," he says. "Don't you see?"

"No, I don't see!" I say trying to pull the knife away.

"Look at me." He grips my jaw with one hand forcing me to look him in the eyes. "You are a goddess, Athena. A true goddess. You healed me. You taught me to see. Truly see. Because of you, I recognize what my real power is as you've mentioned before..." He lets go of my hand on the knife's handle to cup my cheeks. "Sacrifice. Take my life, Athena, as an offering. I offer my life to you. Just promise me that one day you will learn to love again as much as I love you now."

"You love me?" *I can't believe it!*

"Aye," he nods with the most beautiful and brilliant smile I've ever seen.

My breath leaves me. Really, I can't catch my breath. My lungs are refusing to expand around with my collapsing heart because...

I look down at my bloodied hands. I just stabbed myself.

18

WILLIS

*L*ove.
 Stupid. Fucking. Thing. This...
Love.

I don't know how I did not see this coming. I should've known Athena would do this to herself. I know her better than anyone. Better than her parents. Better than I know myself.

She's choking on her own blood and I weep. I wrap my arm around her, pulling her to my chest. With my other arm, I slip my hand beneath her knees and lift. Going out the door, I head down the metal staircase and carry her through Main Street.

"Do you remember our meeting here?" I ask. "You tried to kiss me," I say with a chuckle. "Naughty girl. You've always loved danger."

Athena's arm swings loose, hanging, and I peep down to see her beautiful face. It's as beautiful as it has ever been, aglow by moonlight but motionless. She's gone.

Coddling her lifeless body, I pick up my pace. I remember this road leads to another that will take me to the marina.

To the sea.

Of course, she had to stab herself right in the heart. Right where all things matter most and I regret the way I took her as I did.

There is so much guilt within me, I feel weak. I'm straining to keep Athena's body elevated in my arms. She is so light, but my shame is so heavy.

I fucked her. As usual, I was trying to teach her a lesson and I fucked her when I should've been making love to her. I should've accepted her for who she was. For *what* she was.

A pure creature.

Divine.

I should've allowed her to make her own choices instead of trying to control her and the consequences she knew would come.

Entering the marina, I see a slope where humans take their boats to be lowered into the water.

Heading down the slope, I come near the water's edge. I don't have my powers anymore, but I can still sense the ocean's intentions. I always had a knack for understanding the sea and the sea says she is ready to welcome its new deity.

Placing Athena down, I kneel at her side. The sliver of something in the water stirs, and Lenora pokes her head out. The witch has many limbs. She has made herself look like Orphelius's creature. I cry as I watch Lenora wrap one... two... then three tentacles around Athena, tugging at her ankles and a wrist to pull.

"You knew!" I scowl at the witch. "You knew Athena would not kill Henry."

"Of course, I knew," Lenora smirks. "You weren't the only one who was listening to her fairy tales. Don't you remember the story about the little mermaid? She sacrifices herself for the man she loves. You should've been paying better attention. You should've known this would happen."

"I'm to blame then. Please take me back instead."

"You know I cannot do that. She's made her choice and I will respect her for it."

I wail as Athena is dragged into the depths.

"Stop wailing," Lenora warns. "You sound like a siren. Don't you remember what happens when you sound off a siren at sea?" She waves a finger at me. "You will wake the gods."

Gritting my teeth, "Wake them," I demand. "Wake them all!" I cry out even louder.

Athena's body has mostly disappeared but her head remains above and to my surprise, her eyes flip open!

"Athena!"

She's awakened.

"Willis," she cries but a wrap of sea kelp around her mouth silences her.

I get up, quickly running towards her only to be slowed by a halting barricade of thickening water.

Lenora pulls Athena swiftly and much further out.

"Lenora, bring her back," I yell. "Athena is mine. Bring that woman back to me!"

"Bring her back?" Lenora laughs. "What for? Do you think you'll be able to take better care of her fragility than you did just moments ago? You'll have to do better than that, Captain. And perhaps when you've learned your lesson, you will find your true calling."

Athena squirms.

"Come, girl," Lenora says. "Let me show you what you've really been waiting your whole life to see. Let me show you my *magic*."

For months, I have been coming to sit on the beach. I bring books, a linen bag for sleeping in, and oranges plus a couple of trinkets, including a palm-sized music box—a music player—with an attached speaker that was given to me as a gift from Shelley and Kumiko. I like modern music, especially songs by a lovely lady named GaGa. I can never decide which of her two songs are my most favorite, *Monster* or *The Cure.*

The sheriff has given the three of us, each seaman, a job. Tourists have been swarming in by the busload with all the gossip about the town being cursed with magic. Henry, Orphelius, and I are now Marine Police. We patrol the sea as lawmen, keeping the area safe and void of poaching and other criminal activity. The work is not as tough as when we were in her majesty's navy, but we can get busy. We get especially busy when there are sightings of mystical creatures, reported to be half-man, half-beast.

I, myself, have been diligent in keeping watch for a certain creature. A woman I suspect that has been turned into a half-beast as well.

LOVERS IN DEEP

I've called to her. But she never comes. I don't understand why she doesn't. When Athena was younger, a girl in her teens, she once told me how to summon a mermaid. If Athena had indeed been turned into such a creature, all I'd have to do is simply call to her by her divine name, which I've done thousands of times now. *How much more divine could the name Athena be?* It is, after all, the name of a most famous deity.

I worry that perhaps Athena was not transformed and has been instead taken captive or worse, turned entirely into a sea creature. I try not to think of it. Lenora has assured me Athena is not a slave but has chosen her own path and Lenora refuses to speak with me further about it.

The witch has built herself a clinic, seaside. She enjoys getting involved in human matters. She claims she was a healer in her old life before she was taken from her village when the slave trade was at its peak. She's forged herself a fake doctoral certificate while she learns the ways of modern medicine, although her skills with the trident are genuine. People not only come from far and wide to experience the nostalgia of our town, but they also come to seek miracles from Lenora, come to be known as the Magician of Modern Medicine. With the powers she possesses, Lenora has a knack for curing people deemed incurable.

I wish she'd cure me. I'm lovesick. I was angry with Lenora for a time, but I've come to understand that Lenora is right. She's not in control of my fate.

I am.

There were so many things I could've done differently when it came to Athena. Most often, I think of the first moment I hadn't even known I'd fallen in love with her. Athena reported she had just graduated from school from one level of studies and was going to leave for another type of school. I pitched a few tidal waves and sunk a few atolls that day, and I was miserable for a time. She did not come back for many years.

I could've easily shown myself to her then, but I didn't for the same reason I'm sure she keeps herself hidden from me now.

Because she's ashamed.

Because she's afraid.

She doesn't trust me enough and fears what I'm going to think when I see that she's different.

Tonight, as I cozy up on the beach, propping my head on a makeshift sand pillow, I hear Henry call to me from the beach house.

"Captain!" He stomps, coming down the ramp, swinging his arms with a chilled bottle of homemade beer in his hand.

What a good lad. It's wonderful to drink cold beer. It's even more wonderful to see Henry has use of all his extremities again.

My friend—my *brother*—squats beside me, grinning and watching his own toes wiggle in the sand before he addresses me. "NOAA reports there'll be a swell coming in. There's a hell-of-a-storm above the equator. You might want to move up a bit further on the beach. Get closer to the house or you'll get wet tonight."

NOAA. It stands for National Oceanic and Atmospheric Administration. It's Henry's new *friend* in navigation. I can't quite understand all of the techno-no input, but Henry sure has picked up on it quick. Turns out he's a much finer navigator than I ever was. Although, he's still a pain in the arse, still eager to be in the Captain's favor.

"Or..." he squints his blue eyes at me. "Maybe you should sleep indoors tonight?"

"Don't test me."

"I wasn't testing you."

"Yes, you were."

"For ages, we'd wished we could be men again, and you won't even enjoy the spoils of a few cushions." He holds out his arm towards the beach house.

"I'm not leaving her. Do you remember what it was like to live out there? Alone?"

"Mmm," he nods. "It was lonely, but at least we had each other." He perks up.

"Athena has no one."

Henry slumps, surveying the ocean, turning his head from far left to far right. "Are you sure this is about her and not the sea? Sometimes, I think you're afraid to sleep inside because you're afraid to live on land, you're afraid to be without the thing you loved since *before* Athena."

"Athena is the *only* thing I love. I want to live on land Henry, but not without her. You can understand that, can't you?"

"Yes," he says and spits out a grain of sand that had somehow landed on his lip and made it onto his tongue. "On land or at sea, wherever Shelley is, that's where I want to be."

"Then leave me to my linen bag."

"It's called a sleeping bag."

"Don't be a pain in the arse."

"Aye aye, Captain," he says, with a salute and a nod and then swaps the bottle of beer for one of my oranges.

Bootlicking bastard.

Night inches its way across the sky until the earth appears to be completely covered in darkness. Stars wink and I keep my speaker turned up a bit louder tonight. I put some new songs on my playlist that I want Athena to hear. Love songs. She can pretend not to be listening, but I know what's it's like to live fathoms deep at sea. She can hear me.

Naturally, I'm infuriated when my music box dies!

Ugh! Electricity. It's such a wonderful discovery, but it's not completely reliable.

As I knock my music box against my opposite palm hoping to cause a spark, the wind funnels cold through my ears. The storm to the north is bringing chilled air thousands of miles from the Arctic.

I recall what it was like to be made of water and ice. So stiff and without feeling. But I'm happy to have lived in such a way. I can appreciate everything I touch, everything I smell, everything I taste more than ever...

And now I'm hungry and...

Lonely.

I sit up, unzip my bag to climb free, and walk close to the shore. "Athena!" I call out across the ocean. If I could trade places with her right now, I would. I would go back to the way things were. For her. So she would not have to live this way.

"Athena!" I call out again.

It's been months. Why will she not show herself to me?

Waves roll over my feet and something knocks against my toes. I look down, seeing an odd container of sorts. It's silver-colored, like the bat I was struck with, and the metal is just as dense, strong, and stiff.

Steel is very common in these times.

I pick up the container embellished with fine flowery carvings and turn it around to find an engraving. I have to squint in the dark to see:

Cora Morae
1948 to 2018
Most Beloved Aunt

"Ah, Ms. Morae," I say. "Still not finished with merfolk, are you? I thought Shelley had freed you from your obsessions, your madness, your *curse*."

I turn to the beach house wondering if I should return the urn to Shelley, but a seagull caws to scold me from overhead.

"Yes, okay, my friend," I nod, using as much muscle as I can to unscrew the top.

One second is one second too long to be contained against one's will.

A furious wind blows, but it's warm. The wind comes in from the south, sweeping the ashes from the urn as I pour Cora's remains free so that she will be united with her family and her one true love—the sea.

I rinse the urn and take a look at the inscription once more. Considering the way Shelley has talked of her aunt—as a *nuisance*—I find it very strange that Shelley would include the inscription of *Most Beloved Aunt*. I would not think Shelley would call her aunt such a thing. It's a divine gesture really...

Divine!

I must call to Athena by her most *divine* name.

I drop the urn, searching the vast darkness—both the sky and the ocean—for any hint as to what Athena's divine name would be. Athena is my *most beloved*, but that's not a name and it doesn't feel right to call her that. Not when I just read it on a dead woman's urn. The other seamen use the word, *girlfriend*. It doesn't feel right to call Athena that either. She's no girl.

Athena is also not family, not a relative or even my wife, although she should be, so there is no title I could think to call her other than...

My legs suddenly feel grounded in the sand. I march them into the cool ocean's water. My arms swing and I swear, I've never felt so strong. The thrum of my heart beats with a most heavy and well-paced rhythm and I'm ready to collect what is mine—my true treasure—after all this time.

Slogging through the shallow until I come thigh deep, I

inhale deeply and call out to Athena, calling her by the most divine name only I could give her.

"Lover!" I shout. "Come to me, my love!"

A shadow. The tiniest rounded shadow pops above the surface but a few feet in front of me.

I can't make out visually what I see, but the flick of something...

A fin? It quickly unfolds over the surface with a small splash sinking back into the deep.

Aye, that *was* a fin. A *mermaid's* fin.

"Come, Athena." I stretch out my arms, curling my palms, signaling. "Lover, come to me."

19

ATHENA

I don't want to go. Not to him. Not to the man who resisted me for most of my life. I see now he was trying to protect me from this realm, but I refused to heed his warnings and look at me now.

I am possessed by magic.

"Come," he calls. His voice is irresistible. Like bait, it lures me.

I'm trying to resist but a hunger—a *need*—to flutter my fin and get closer is driving me towards him.

I'm a *fish*, circling the baited hook knowing well there's danger in front of me. But still, I move closer because there is nothing more intriguing in all this vastness than what is right in front of me.

He smiles, waving me towards him.

Oh, dear gods. He is magnificent. The memory of him in my bed makes me ache more now than I did when I was a teenager, wondering what it would be like to be with him.

Have him.

But I can't have him. Not like this. And I don't want him to see me like this either—half covered in *scales*. He's been transformed back into something beautiful. I, on the other hand, have been transformed into something bizarre and horrible.

"Lover," he sings, treading towards me.

His voice casts what feels like an invisible net and I'm struggling to swim away.

He comes closer. Water sloshes around me as he makes his approach. His hands find my shoulders, gripping, and I don't fight. It would be useless. Willis caught me long before he ever even touched me.

"Athena," he growls, pulling me to him. "Why have you been avoiding me?"

Pulling my head back with a fist of my hair, he kisses me. His flesh is salted and cool from the winds while his kiss is hot.

I push away, pouting. "Stop, Willis. I wasn't avoiding you. I was avoiding..." I flick my fin, looking down at the deformity that is my cage.

Willis and I can never be together, not as long as I am in this form, not in the way I know he needs, the way a man needs to be with his woman.

He lifts my chin, sweeping his thumb across my lips. A smile hints through his voice. "You know damn well you could *never* avoid me. We are like the earth and sea, you and me. Two bodies that can never be separated."

He picks me up. If I could kick I would, but I have no legs. I wiggle but I stop, feeling silly like a fish flipping exaggeratedly after it's been hooked and plucked from the water.

"Willis, you don't want this," I tell him. "You don't want me. You have legs now. You deserve more. You deserve better."

"Strange," he says, squeezing tighter, dragging my lower half as he treads towards the sand. "I remember I used to think the same thing about you."

Willis brings me to shore where he sits, cradling me in his arms. I nuzzle my face into his chest to hide my shame, hoping he's not looking at me too critically. He nudges me back and takes off his shirt.

Shamelessly, I stare at his chest and I notice a trinket hanging from around his neck. He slips the trinket over his head to hold it up, dangling a golden compass above me.

I blink, recognizing the treasure with magical powers, powers I can already feel working through my spine.

A tingle in my lower back shoots through my tail. As Willis opens the chain from which the compass hangs to place it over my head, the tingle becomes a shock, and the shock brings crushing pain.

"Ugh," I gurgle as the single column of bones running through my tail shatters.

Clawing into Willis, I confess, "It hurts," feeling the lower portion of my body tear right down the middle as if I'm being ripped in half.

"Shh," Willis coos, trying to calm me. He strokes my hair and rubs my back, planting kisses sweetly over my cheeks and neck.

Only, his touch seems to make the ache easier to bare. "Hold me," I beg. "Kiss me more. Cover me," I request as if Willis could shield me from this pain.

Quickly, I am rolled onto my back. My body, transforming, lands flush against the sand. My mouth is the first to be covered by Willis's lips along with his tongue as the rest of him slowly rolls like a warm wave on top of me.

My tail finally splits completely and the shattered bones, once a single extension of my spine, collect to become leg bones.

Willis breaks our kiss to peep down at our lower halves. He's straddled over my thighs.

"Make love to me," I say, "before the magic goes away."

Sure, I'm wearing the compass which should allow me to stay in this form, but I don't want to risk this moment getting away from us.

And neither does he.

Willis's button and zipper come undone. His pants are barely down his ass before he's upon me again, splitting my legs apart with his knees. He glides the tip of his erection along my slit, barely dipping, checking to see if I'm wet. He coats his cock with my arousal before he sinks himself into me.

Fully, he drives his thick hook within me as his hands glide and grab along the contour of my body while he grunts and moans.

He kisses me deeper than he's ever kissed me before. I feel like I'm drowning. Into my core from both openings—between my legs and at my mouth—he is plunging, taking my breath away.

With each grind of his hips against my groin, I feel his rough curls rake against my heated flesh. My core tightens which makes his cock throb, pulsing thicker and longer within me.

He groans as I fist his hair and wrap my legs tight around his waist. His body caves, his abs constricting tighter and tighter with each thrust, as he works his length repeatedly deep and hard.

Somehow, I manage to pull him in deeper. My hands wrap behind his back, squeezing, and I'm jolting in unison with the rhythm of his pleasuring thrusts.

"Mmm," he growls, slowing down to nibble at my chin, my collarbone, and then my nipple.

My back arches and my hips buck with the overwhelming stimulus connecting with my clit. Pulling and tugging, lapping and sucking, his mouth is working wonders at my breast as he manages to burden my core with his cock.

"I'm going to flood you," he says. His voice is low and intense, like a warning.

My jaw, so tight, unhinges as both of his hands make their way behind my back and towards the nape of my neck where he pulls at my hair, exposing my neck to him. He buries his face while his hips thrust with even more power.

Our friction burns. His length is deep and his thickness is splitting me apart.

But his power consumes and excites me.

Ecstasy is within my grasp. Like magic, its elusive power lingers and I want it badly. Desperately. *This* is the magic I want to possess me. I want Willis to possess me. I want him to own me but he's not the type to take what he wants so I'm going to have to give myself to him.

"Drown me," I say, clamping tight around him.

Gripping beneath my knees, he flexes, lifts, and spreads my legs wider, so he can slam into me again and again.

The crest... I feel it coming.

Solid and with great force, he crashes into me and, like a wave, my orgasm smashes—*clobbering me*—and washes over me to leave my body tingling from the crown of my head to the tips of my toes.

Willis grunts as he shoots against my inner walls, flooding my cavern to coat my inner cave with his semen.

His muscles twitch as we both relax and I stroke my hands up his sides. My eyes follow my fingers as they trace his dewy skin until they make their way up to the top of his chiseled chest and I make eye contact with him.

He's grinning and I turn my head away bashfully.

"Aye, come now," he says, grabbing my jaw and turning my head to face him. "You can look. This is always what you wanted to see, isn't it?"

I can feel my eyes getting glossy as I look him over. *I'm such a freak!* With or without legs, I'm still a freak when it comes to him because I'm just as fascinated as if I was still a child. He's so beautiful and I'm still so... *me*. I worry if he really feels as in love with me as I am with him.

"Willis, do you—"

"I love you," he says, rolling to his side, bringing me with him until he is on his back and I am resting on top. "Forever you are mine now. I don't own you, but you still belong to me. Aye?" He lifts my chin to lock eyes with me.

"Aye."

He smiles, scrubbing some sand free from my shoulders before he tightens his arms around me and nuzzles a kiss, rubbing his lips back and forth and then puckering his lips to suck at my forehead. The gesture is cute and it makes me giggle.

"What are you laughing at?" he scowls.

"What was that?"

"What?"

"That!" I point to my forehead. "Was that a kiss?"

"What's the matter? You don't like that?" He puckers his mouth, making fishy lips.

I plant my chin on his chest shaking my head with a smile.

"Would you rather I pant like a dog?" He sticks his tongue out panting and I glower.

"I had no idea you were so strange."

"Strange?" He squints one eye, furrowing his brows, and he swats my bare ass! "I'm completely human." Willis tickles me, making me squirm. "I've even kept my eyes and everything and *now* you think I'm strange."

I bury my face in his chest, mumbling, "Do *you* think *I'm* strange?"

"Yes," he says and my breath hitches as the chambers of my heart cease to open and close with such a painful revelation. "You were a strange girl who grew to be an even stranger woman, but lucky for you, I'm accustomed to strange things." He grabs my bottom and squeezes. "And you, my love, are unlike anything to have ever lived on this earth or beyond. *You* are the magical, rare treasure every adventurer seeks." He lifts the compass to his lips, kissing the trinket. "*You* are my most beloved of all things." Another kiss comes to my mouth. "Am I also *your* most beloved?" he asks.

"Yes."

"Aye, see. Then you must be strange to love a man like me."

Music plays from the interior of the beach house and I look up to see the other couples inside are wide awake and dancing.

"Do you want to go in?" I ask.

"Later," he says. "I want to enjoy the spoils of all we've conquered together."

Seemingly content, Willis closes his eyes to rest while sprawling his limbs wide across the sand. Like a starfish, he spreads himself out, flat across the beach, except for one arm which he keeps wrapped around my back.

Pressing my ear to his chest, I listen for Willis's heart. I close my eyes, also content, when I hear his human heart beating.

Months Later...

Tap, tap, tap. I glower at the creature behind the glass. *Tap, tap, tap.* I bang the tip of my finger a bit harder this time.

"He doesn't like that," says the receptionist, a silvering brunette, behind the counter.

"Who doesn't?" I ask with a devious smile.

"The critter in the tank," she replies and goes back to typing.

I peek back into the glass at the animal trapped in the aquarium. I wonder how long Lenora plans to keep Levi locked up in there and as a fish or... *whatever* the hell he is. He has arms and legs plus a tail but his oversized head is spearheaded with his mouth, surrounded by tiny tentacles placed under him. It appears he must sift through rocks for food.

"Serves you right, bottom feeder."

I tap on the glass again when I jerk back! Levi has speared his head into the glass.

I'd like to spear him with a knife! "Why you little shi—"

"Athena," calls Lenora. "I'm ready for you now."

I look up. The doctor looks lovely today. She's wearing

slacks, which I know she loves wearing pants, with a bright red shirt under her white coat. Her hair is down and I love the tiny curls, which seem to have grown substantially longer since just last week. I wish I had her powers to make myself look that good in so little time.

"How are you?" she asks.

"I'm good," I answer, although my nerves are firing off like crazy as I follow Lenora out of the waiting room, past her receptionist, and down a short hall where we find ourselves in an examination room painted of sea life.

She rolls the ultrasound machine over as I hop up on the cushiony covered exam table. "Lift your shirt and pull the waistline of your pants down below your belly and lie back," she says.

My hands are shaking. I do as she instructs swiftly, so Lenora won't suspect that I'm scared.

"I know you're afraid," Lenora says, smiling.

I forgot, she can read my mind. Even with the compass around my neck, allowing me to live on land with legs, I'm still somewhat of a sea beast.

"It's okay," Lenora nods her head. "This isn't going to hurt."

"But what if my baby..." I choke. *What if my baby is a freak? What if my baby comes out deformed?*

"We'll deal with whatever comes our way," Lenora replies, squirting clear jelly on my belly as she sits.

She tucks a towel over my pants and under my shirt. I suspect it is to protect my clothing from the gel. Placing the head of the ultrasound wand on top of my stomach, Lenora presses firmly, taps a few buttons on the keyboard, and then moves the wand around firmly.

Minutes seem to pass. She's not saying anything. Sweat is beginning to bead at my forehead and I'm about to *snap* when Willis enters the room.

"Sorry, I'm late," he flips off his navy-blue baseball cap to reveal his cropped haircut, which he hates. But Pike, his boss, insists on short hair. The cap matches his uniform with the words, MARINE POLICE, printed across the front. He kisses me before he slides the cap over my head. "Everything okay?"

I smile up at him but roll my eyes over to Lenora. "She hasn't said anything yet."

"Because I'm not done." She hits a few more keys.

"Is there something wrong?" I'm beginning to panic. "There must be something wrong. Clearly, there's something wrong if you're not saying anything."

"Whoa." Willis strokes the small tendrils of hair away from my upper lip that are beginning to stick because I'm perspiring. "Give the witch a minute to work."

Lenora stops what she's doing to flash Willis a wicked glance. "I'm not a witch. I'm a—"

"Healer," interrupts Willis. "Yes, yes. My apologies."

Lenora's demeanor instantly changes. "Are you ready, Athena?"

"Ready? Ready for what?"

There's a twinkle in Lenora's eyes. "For this?"

A swishing sound cuts through the room. The sound is quick, fast-paced, and even.

"Is that my..." I have no words to express the joy I feel. "Is that my..."

"That's your baby's heart."

Salted tears flow from my eyes and I cover my face in a giddy reaction. My hands are quickly removed, however, as Willis pulls my hands away to kiss me. "That's our baby," he says. Our eyes connect and we kiss again.

But I stiffen as does he. We've discussed what we need to ask, which is the baby's sex and health.

"She's healthy," Lenora replies. Of course, she already knows what we were going to ask.

Turning the ultrasound screen towards us so Willis and I can see, Lenora points out our baby's head, arms, hands, and legs.

Yes, legs!

"Don't get too excited," Lenora interrupts our state of joy.

"I *knew* there was going to be something wrong." I am beside myself with more worry than I've had since finding out I was pregnant.

Of course, there's something wrong with my baby, but it's going to be okay. I'm still going to love her. I'm still going to take care of her. Magic, the mystics, the gods—they will not have their way with her. Willis and I, we will protect her and she will know love through all the days of her life no matter what.

"There's nothing wrong with her, Athena." Lenora shuffles, keeping her butt planted and scooting herself along the slick floors with her rolling chair towards a drawer to pull out a trinket. "She's just... mmm... *different*."

"Diffffferent?" The hesitation in Willis's voice makes me glad I'm not the only one worried.

"She'll need to wear this," replies Lenora, dangling the trinket in front of me. "But only when she wants to keep legs when she's *in* the water."

I hold out my palm, watching as Lenora plops a little anchor—a pendant—made of gold in my palm.

"My gift to you and your child," she says.

Suddenly, I am at ease. Lenora already knew the shape our child was going to be in—half-shaped by Willis and half-shaped by me. So, of course, there's nothing wrong with my baby and I should've never doubted that anything but perfection—a perfect fairy tale—would come from Willis and I, together.

Willis peeks in my palm, closes my hand to clutch the anchor within, and squeezes. Tears are about to pour from his eyes.

"Have you picked out a name?" asks Lenora.

"We've decided on Azure," croaks Willis, wiping his wet face and standing up straight. "Since it's a girl."

"Azure?" Lenora raises a brow.

"Mhm," Willis replies. "It means *blue*."

"Yes, Azure." Lenora plants her hands over her heart. "What a perfect name for a most beloved little mermaid."

EPILOGUE

AZURE

Fifteen Years Old...
Wind blows from the north. The pages of my sketchbook lift at the corners and I press them down noticing I've made an unwanted line along the cloud that I'm drawing.

Flipping over my pencil, I start to erase and the wind blows more heavily across my face. My auburn hair gets stuck in my mouth, so I brush the tendrils free as well as from my stormy gray eyes. While swiveling my head, I see the group of teenagers, my classmates, down the beach still having a great time.

I really wish they'd hurry up and leave.

The sun is nearly about to set and from the look of their skins—*burnt*—I'm sure they've been here all day. But I guess that's what it's like to be cool, to have friends, to not be so... *different*. Time just seems to fly by when you're having fun.

I hate them.

I hate the way they fumble over each other. The way they taunt and tease one another—*flirting*. That group likes to play a lot of Truth or Dare. They even do it at school and it grosses me out to think how much spit has been swapped between them.

Oh, no! He's looking at me again.

Trip. That's his nickname. That's what everyone calls him, although I think it hardly suits him compared to his *real* name, Theseus, which is the name of the most famous hero in Greek mythology.

Flipping my hair off my shoulder, I go back to my drawing. Beneath a cloud, I'm tempted to draw an image of Trip. *Again*. Already six feet tall with broad shoulders, long limbs, and lean muscle, I suspect Trip will eventually outgrow the lanky teen look to become anatomically perfect, except for the huge scar over his torso.

I peep back to get a better look at him. Trip has his mother's hair—a beautiful blond that shines gold. He has her eyes as well—big, blue, and wide like the ocean. People say he also has a heart like hers, too—overly compassionate. His mother, Yanka, is a nurse known to hoard animals. Apparently, Trip hoards a lot of critters as well so it's not surprising he's brought a few dogs with him to hang out amongst his friends.

I'm sorry to say, I hate the dogs because they *know* I'm different. They like to spy on me as much as their owner does, but at least they keep their distance.

The dogs howl in delight at Trip's friends as everyone leaps and splashes, playing in the small waves rolling in. Trip, however, doesn't go anywhere near the water. He just stands around, kicking the sand, stretching his arms, bending this way and that, as if he's contemplating or perhaps gathering the courage to get in the water, but he doesn't go in.

Considering what he went through this past summer, I don't blame him.

He turns his head my way and I find myself caught in his gaze until he pivots and marches my way.

Oh crap!

Quickly, I shuffle with my things. Closing my notebook, I slide it under my butt to sit on it. I smooth my wild hair down my face, sit crisscross, and clutch my pencil in my lap.

As Trip approaches with confidence, swinging his arms, the sand flying out from behind his heels as he makes his way to me, I see his scar. Like a rainbow turned sideways, the enormous bite mark fans over his chest and abdomen reaching into his groin where I cannot see the end, despite the low hanging waistline of his surf shorts.

"Hey," he says. His two feet halt right next to me.

"Hi." My eyes blink up as my head tilts way back to see the young man, a sophomore in high school like me, towering above.

"Would you mind if I sit?" He points to the sand where his toes are wiggling just two inches from me.

Between the columns that are his legs, I see his friends have all stopped playing. Like ducks in a pond, they bob with each wave, spying on us.

"Don't mind them," he says and plants his butt in the sand, propping his knees up where he rests his forearms. I want to mirror his action, so I can catch my breath. He's more gorgeous up close than he is from far away and I have an urge to pant.

I inhale slowly. He smells good, like coconut (probably from his sunscreen) mixed with spicy cologne. Of all the beaches I've visited, I can honestly say Trip smells the most exotic of any tropical paradise.

"Can I... do you... is there something I can do for you?" I ask.

I don't know why he's come to sit next to me. He's tried talking to me before, but I ignore him. As popular as he is, I figure he just wants to tease me like a lot of my classmates often do usually as one of their dares.

"Nah, I just..." Our eyes lock for a moment before he looks at my legs.

I gather my knees in my arms, pulling my legs to my chest. "If you're here to poke fun at me—"

"That's not why I'm here." The natural pout of his mouth disappears as he grins. "You looked like you could use some company. If you'd rather be alone..."

Puppy dog eyes, which I've never seen so cute before, blink.

"It's fine," I mutter.

"Cool." He sits and points to the ocean. "You swim?"

"Rarely," I lie. "How about you? Are you not planning to surf today?" I've seen him surfing many times—for years. He's very good.

"Nah," he says lowly, picking up sand and throwing it.

"Is that because of..." I point to his scar.

"Yeah." He bites his bottom lip as his shoulders shrug. "I miss it though. I miss surfing a lot."

"So why don't you take a board out?"

"The attack, I guess," he says, locking eyes with me again.

"You shouldn't be afraid to go back out there. The likelihood that you'll get bitten by a shark a second time... I'm sure it won't happen again."

He bows his chin. "It's still possible."

Unfortunately, it *is* still possible. Lenora allows the beasts of the sea to be free except when she needs their help to heal someone.

"What's that?" I ask, pointing to the necklace hanging around Trip's neck.

"It's a shark tooth. Lenora gave it to me after the attack. Lenora is so weird, you know?"

"Oh, I know."

"But I trust her, so I still want to wear it for some reason.

She said it would help me keep perspective and maybe lead me to the cure I seek."

"Cure? Cure for what?"

He takes the necklace off and dangles it in front of me. "My fear."

I put out my hand where he drops the tooth into my palm.

"That's a little strange, giving someone a shark tooth to wear after they were attacked."

Trip lifts the anchor at my neck. "Can I see yours?"

Reluctantly, I lift the golden pendant over my head and hand it over, but I do it quickly. I don't want him to see the gooseflesh that's risen in reaction to the slight brush of his fingers.

"How about you?" He squints one eye at me, slipping my own necklace over his head, making me uneasy. "There's a rumor that's been going around since day one of kindergarten that you got this charm from Lenora as well, and it keeps you from..." He clears his throat. "Turning into a mermaid."

I loosen my palm. I've just pierced my skin. I had no idea I'd been clutching his shark tooth so tightly. "That's ridiculous."

"Is it?" He squints his other eye at me.

"Yes, it is." I hug my legs tighter, planting my cheek on my knees.

"Hey, Trip!" shouts one of his friends. "We're leaving. Sun's gone down."

"That's cool, man. I'm going to stay here for a bit. You guys go on ahead," he yells back.

"Maybe you should go with your friends," I encourage.

"Maybe I want to stay a while longer." He picks up some sand and throws the grains at my legs.

I scoop a big handful and throw some sand back, which

crash lands against his taut pecks to bounce and sprinkle over his entire body.

He spits, scraping his hands adorably over his tanned cheeks and sun kissed lips.

"Hey, you got some in my face," he grumbles, spitting.

I laugh. "Maybe you shouldn't throw sand."

"Maybe you shouldn't be so cute. Are you going to the homecoming dance?"

My breath hitches. *What did he just ask?*

"I wasn't planning on... I don't... no."

"You wanna be my date? I mean... can I take you as my date?"

"I'm not really sure," I say. I've never been asked on a date before, and I was sure no one ever would. "I'll have to ask my parents, especially my dad."

"I'm sure it'll be cool. Our dads work together."

Our dads *do* work together—*sorta*. My dad works in marine police enforcement. His dad is the deputy.

"If you feel more comfortable, I can ask your dad *for* you."

"*You* would ask my dad to take me to the dance?"

"Mhm," he nods.

Jeez, Trip is brave. Even I have a hard time confronting my father. The man is just so... so...

"My father is really old school." *And I mean "old school," as in from the 1700s old school.*

"That's cool. I'll talk to him." Trip rakes his fingers through his blond hair, shaking the sand I threw at him loose. "Hey, let's go for a swim." He gets up on his feet, putting his hand out to me.

I panic! "Right now? I thought you said you were afraid of the water."

"Not water. *Sharks*. But I'm feeling brave right now. Come on. Let's go in."

"I can't. No." *He's wearing my pendant!*

LOVERS IN DEEP

"What's the matter? Are you afraid you're going to grow a fin or something?"

He doesn't seriously think I'd turn into a mermaid, does he? Even though I would.

"It's getting dark, Trip. Maybe we should go home."

He sighs, sitting back down next to me. His dogs, who have been sniffing up and down the shore, make an approach, but he whistles to shoo them away.

"They really listen to you," I say. "Do they do everything you ask?"

"Pretty much."

"That's impressive."

"Not as impressive as having fins."

I take a breath. "Trip, whatever crazy idea you have about me—"

"I happen to have a *lot* of crazy ideas about you, Azure. Why do you always keep to yourself?"

I'm regretting the idea of going to homecoming with him. "Why are you always trying to talk to me?"

"Why do you always look so blue?"

"I'm not blue."

"Mysterious, then. It adds to your allure."

"I'm not alluring."

"Okay, just pretty as ffffuuhh..." He bites his lip and throws more sand. "Listen, I just wanted to talk. Does being a mermaid give you superpowers? Can you read my mind?" His blue eyes shine like sapphires as he licks his lips. "Do you know what thoughts I'm having about you right now?"

I ignore what he's asking. I don't need superpowers to know what he's thinking. But I *do* know I'm *not* the girl for him, especially since I'm only *half* a girl sometimes.

"Can I have my pendant back?" I put out my palm, holding his shark tooth. "Please, I'd really like my anchor back now."

"Yeah, sure," he says lowly, slowly pulling the anchor off over his head.

Trip places the anchor next to the tooth in my palm and the second he has his own necklace in his fingers, he throws it.

Into the air the tooth floats until it lands back in the sea from where it came. It makes a ripple.

Out of nowhere, a wave comes towards us, crashing hard onto the shore with its edge fanning and jetting speedily towards us. I yelp as I scoot back as fast as I can before the water's edge reaches my toes. Thankfully, the water recedes, and I can breathe.

I almost grew a fin in front of Trip!

"Wow, look at that," he says, reaching over my legs to pick up the shark tooth that was brought back by the wave.

"Yes, I see." My pulse quickens.

"Lenora said the tooth would lead me to a cure." He leans in. "What do you think she meant by that?" He nudges me with his elbow.

"I don't know." Dangling the anchor from my hand, I open the chain to place it back over my head before another wave rolls in and Trip will literally trip over himself when he sees who—or *what*—I really am.

Trip clutches my hand over the anchor before I can slip my head through the loop.

"Azure, look at me. You can trust me." He rubs his forehead. "Everyone wants to talk to me about what happened during the attack, but I can't even look at myself. What do you think when you see this?" Trip scrolls his hand flat down his chest over the scar left by a great white shark, which my father says had to be nearly forty feet long.

My father was the first of emergency responders on the beach when Trip was attacked, and I recall what my father had to say about the condition Trip was in: "The boy should've been torn to shreds. Only a true son of Poseidon could have wrestled his way free of such a magnificent beast and survived."

I rub my legs. "Trip? You think you're different, don't you?"

"I don't think. I know," he says boldly.

"Do you recall what happened to you when you were attacked?"

"N-n-no," he stutters as I get up to strip down my clothes. I keep my bikini on, but the bottom will have to eventually come off.

"What *do* you remember?"

"I just remember pain and struggling."

"Do you remember fighting the shark at all?"

He shakes his head and I put out my palm, wiggling my fingers to encourage him to take my hand before his eyes pop out of their sockets.

"Lenora was right to lead you to me, but I'm not the cure you seek and you're not afraid of sharks either. In fact, I think you're afraid of the same thing that I am."

"And what's that?" he says, gripping my fingers to stand up.

I lead him to stand beside me before an open ocean. "We are afraid to see ourselves unlike other people."

"I admit I'm not as afraid with you standing next to me," he says.

"I must admit I'm scared to death of what you're going to think when you see the *real* me."

Trip tugs on my chin and I face him. "No matter what, I promise I'm still taking you to homecoming."

"Oh, Trip." I smile. "This *is* your homecoming."

"Well, good." He leans in to kiss me.

Fireworks! Shooting stars! Sparks!

They all go off around me.

"That was unexpected," I say. "What was that for?"

"I don't know. Just in case we get eaten by sharks or something." He jokes. "Hey, Azure, do you want to get a pizza and watch a movie instead?"

My heart flutters. "Is that what *you* want to do?"

"Not really, no. I'd rather go back to where we were sitting and make out, but I'm aware your uncles patrol the beaches this time of night. I'd rather face a shark again than one of them."

I slap Trip in the chest and he grabs me, tickling.

We land in the sand and we talk for some time. "Time," he says is the one thing his father preaches should never go to waste. "A man could possess eternity and still not find enough time to spend with his loved ones."

Trip lets me touch his scar. I let him help loosen my bikini bottom.

The next thing I know, my anchor has slipped free from my grasp and I'm hooking my arms around his neck. Swiftly, he pulls until we are waist deep in the ocean swapping spit and sharing kisses.

The End

DEDICATION

Thank you for reading this final installment of The Sea Men series.

This trilogy is dedicated to three courageous men who confessed their dreams to me and changed my perception of anchovies with jalapenos pizza.

Please consider leaving your honest review.

For more books by Dani Stowe and my other pen names, visit BabeFuelBooks.com

Made in United States
Orlando, FL
04 August 2022